Vernice

Book 2 in the Women of the Fellowship Series

Julia A. Royston

Edited by: Claude R. Royston

BK Royston Publishing
Jeffersonville, IN

BK Royston Publishing
P. O. Box 4321
Jeffersonville, IN 47131
502-802-5385
http://www.bkroystonpublishing.com
bkroystonpublishing@gmail.com

Cover Photo: Jonathan Snorten
Cover Design: Bill Lacy

ISBN-13: 978-0692705438
ISBN-10: 0692705430

Printed in the United States of America

Dedication

I dedicate this book to every single mother who is striving every day to raise her children on her own to the best of her ability. Putting her children first is her priority and choice, but with the eternal hope that parental obligation will not keep her from the desire of the romantic love that lies deep in her heart.

Acknowledgements

First, I acknowledge my Lord and Savior Jesus Christ for giving me all of my gifts and especially my gift to write His words.

My husband who is always supportive, loving and encouraging me to utilize all of my gifts and talents. Thank you honey.

To my mother, Dr. Daisy Foree, who is my best friend, number one cheerleader and always tells me, "hang in there, you can do it." To my father, Dr. Jack Foree, who is never far away from me in spirit and in my heart. I only have to look in the mirror each day to see him.

To Rev. Claude and Mrs. Lillie Royston who support me in everything I do. Especially, Rev. Royston for his careful eye to detail and his sensitive heart to content.

To the rest of my family, I love you and thank you for your prayers, support and love.

Introduction

In Book 1 of the Women of the Fellowship Series we were introduced to Jillian Forrester, Vernice Washington and Erma Jamison. These three women are different in their looks, occupation and residences but simultaneously, they are alike in that they all three want to be loved.

In Book 2, Vernice is a single mother of a high school senior about to go to college on a full athletic scholarship. Vernice and her son live in windy Chicago going about their daily lives. Vernice works hard at her job striving to get ahead and be promoted. David, Jr. works hard at school wanting to make his mother proud and himself independent.

They attend church and very active in the national organization, The Christian Church World Fellowship Conference. Vernice works on the national planning staff and would love to meet a very nice, Christian man and eventually remarry. Vernice didn't really want a stepfather for her son because his biological father wasn't a good father.

Now that her son is almost fully grown, she doesn't have to worry about a stepfather for her son, but her desire is only for passionate love in her life.

Julia Royston

Table of Contents

Vernice

Chapter 1

Anyone who has ever been in a relationship of any kind for any length of time knows that you never tell everything that happened. No amount of therapy, girls' night out, friends or family will ever know everything that happened. Some things a person keeps to themselves. Some things can't be uttered. It is too painful and hurtful to the ears to hear again. You don't want the brain to recall it from its secure storage place. The demeaning language, the negative comparisons, the humiliating sexual requests and physical abuse that can exist in a relationship. The walls of the apartment, house or condo know exactly what happened. If only the furniture, dishes and other household accoutrements could stand witness to the many acts of disrespect and degradation that were imposed on one person by another. At one time, this same space saw love, laughter and much

1

joy. There was care, cuddling and courtesy displayed easily in this same living space. One day something happened. The room was introduced to someone new. The body, face and voice was the same, but the words coming out of that familiar face were completely different. There were introductions to unlawful characters, erratic behavior, insults flung, and threats of abandonment while unquestionable allegiance was demanded at any cost. What would it cost? How much would one person have to pay for love? How much would one person have to sacrifice to be appreciated, acknowledged and adored? What would have to be spent to actually have a child's father spend time with someone that was a biological and genetic result of their DNA? Dignity had left the building and intimidation had taken its place. Love could not make its way home, but sent fear, apprehension and worry to abide instead.

Vernice

Vernice hurried into the house and pushed the button to close the garage door. She still had her purse and groceries for dinner still in her arms. A mother can always multi-task and use her entire body to get the job done. After leaning the grocery bags up against the door frame, she was able to open the kitchen door with her one free hand. Vernice felt something hard and metal scrape her lower right leg. She looked down and found three suitcases on the kitchen floor just to the left of the garage door. She almost stumbled over them but missed them because she went to the left to put the bags on the counter instead of to the right where the suitcases were clearly in her path. When the bags were safely on the counter, Vernice thought, 'why are suitcases in the floor? Where is David, Sr. going?' Panic and fear suddenly began dropping hints of the passenger on the trip being her instead of David, Sr. Vernice thought, 'Is David throwing me out? He wouldn't leave the house that he insisted was his, but has barely helped make mortgage payments in the past six months or never cleaned up because that was a woman's work. He also hasn't bothered to come home before midnight the past three months.'

Vernice heard David Sr.'s footsteps coming down the hallway and toward the kitchen. Seeing Vernice in the kitchen doorway, David, Sr. appeared startled.

"Oh, you are home," David said matter-of-factly and dropped his eyes. He moved toward the three suitcases and put some items in one bag. In the other hand, he held a large envelope along with his keys.

"Yes, I'm home. Where are you going?" Vernice asked.

A huge knowing smile came over David, Sr.'s face, "Well, vile Vernice. I am going where I don't have

Vernice

to tolerate you anymore. I have been given an opportunity of a lifetime. I am leaving Chicago and going to California. I can't take this city, you or this life any more. There's a new place, job, life and hopefully, a brand new gorgeous wife waiting for me. I'm out," David said as he threw the envelope and keys on the counter. "I wrote this note, but now it is unnecessary." David tore up the note and tossed it on the counter while he rechecked his luggage.

Vernice stood near the toaster and could see her reflection in the metal. She knew she wasn't ugly, but would be considered plain Jane at the least. Vernice had a model's build with only a very slight protruding stomach as a result of the birth of her son. Vernice stood five foot nine with good posture as her mother had taught her. She wore very little makeup only splurging on lip gloss and pressing powder for special occasions. Vernice's clothes were suits and dresses of very conservative colors. She mostly wore black, brown and navy blue with solid colored blouses to match. While other women spent hundreds of dollars on couture accessories, Vernice stuck with the store brand purses that were functional in the colors of her clothes, black, brown and navy.

This day, Vernice's black purse was half way on the counter and suddenly crashed to the ground along with this hoax of a marriage. Vernice made no sudden moves or attempt to stop David, Sr. from leaving. Deep down, she wanted him to leave as fast as possible. She shouldn't have cared what he was about to do next, but just had to ask.

"What are you going to do with the wife you have now?" Vernice asked and waited for an answer.

David, Sr. turned to her and said, "A divorce as fast as a lawyer can get it done. Listen, Vernice, you are a great mother to our son and a wonderful

Vernice

housekeeper. I won't take any of that away from you, but you bore me to tears and bring out the worst in me. I am not attracted to you, don't desire you, don't love you and have no interest in you. I should be sorry for all of the horrible things I have done and said, but I am not. You're still here so I'm leaving."

"So I was good enough to marry four years ago, have your baby, but not good enough to remain your wife because I'm boring?" Vernice pushed.

"That's exactly what I am saying. I don't know what I was thinking by marrying you. You caught me at a point of weakness. I thought that you would change to keep up with me, but I was wrong. I should have left you with our baby. Having that baby is your greatest achievement. Look at your girl Jillian. She is heavy, on the plump side or big boned but at least, she knows what clothes to put on all of that meat she got," David said not caring how Vernice felt.

"You've been checking out my girl too?" Vernice couldn't believe it. Her world was literally spinning out of control.

"Yep, she's a lot to check out too for a big girl, she's pretty, smart, can sing her butt off and one day she'll be rich and going places. Where are you going, Vernice? You work a low end five figure salary job with a four year old." David, Sr. picked up the first two suitcases with one hand and opened the door to the garage with the other. He pushed the button and the garage door went up.

Vernice walked quickly to the garage doorway and yelled, "What am I supposed to tell our son? He's four, but he's not stupid! One day his dad is here and the next he's not!" Vernice went back in the kitchen to grab something to defend herself just in case David, Sr. attacked.

Vernice

This time, David, Sr. came in the kitchen calm so she braced herself up against the counter with a small knife in her right hand and waited for the inevitable. It didn't happen. David, Sr.'s stance was relaxed and he finally said, "He's young Vernice. Tell him anything you want. I died or I left. You choose. You have full custody now. You are not getting any money out of me because you have plenty money. It's stashed away in that precious 401K of yours."

Vernice's head was about explode, but she still had one piece of her mind left. She put down the knife, got a piece of paper from her portfolio and a pen. David, Sr. was taking the last suitcase in his hand and Vernice grabbed him by the arm. The sudden move caught him off guard since his hands were full. He pushed her hard in the stomach with the suitcase and she fell back onto the floor. Laying on the floor, Vernice begged him, "Sign this paper, you black..." She didn't usually curse and it almost slipped out, but what she felt about him would be left unsaid.

David, Sr. made no move toward Vernice, but stood at the door and said, "I'm not signing anything for you. The divorce papers are signed along with the lawyer's name, address and number in that envelope on that counter. My signature on those divorce papers is the last signature you will ever see of mine. You sign them and mail them in. Don't ever try to contact me again for anything." He walked out the door leaving it ajar.

The last thing she heard was the car door close and the garage door lower. Vernice laid there on the floor crying tears of sadness, anger and regret. She realized that she should have walked away sooner, but she was hard headed and too stubborn to go home to her wonderful parents who would have gladly taken her and David, Jr. in. She was angry that such a sweet little boy would not have a good father in his life. She was now left with a four year old, a mortgage and a month of unpaid bills. After hours on that floor, she got up, picked up the items from her purse along with the pieces of her life.

Fourteen years had passed since that awful Friday. Vernice's heart and soul were changed forever. Her approach to life, career, love and future was all new as a result of that day. Unbeknownst to Vernice, she had built walls, fences and doors to protect her emotions, but recently they were screaming 'let us out!'

On this Friday, Vernice was walking into the same kitchen through that same garage door. She turned on the light and there were no suitcases, noise, fear or anxiety just peace and quiet. Her son was at her mother's house. Vernice was tired from her day and was still recovering from a week spent at a church conference. She was putting her groceries away when a familiar number appeared on her phone.

She answered it quickly, "Hello."

"Hey girl. I am just calling to check on you and see how your week went," Jillian Forrester sounded glad to hear Vernice's voice but tired as well.

Jillian Forrester had been Vernice's best friend for more than 30 years. They were church kids with mothers who were best friend who attended church conferences all over the country and now they were the national coordinators of this same conference.

"You've got great timing. I just got in the house. How are you doing? You sound more tired than I am," Vernice said as she sat down at her kitchen table.

"I am tired. I'm still trying to recover from everything. I'm tired, happy, disappointed, mad, sad, in love and disgusted all at the same time," Jillian said as she sat down on the couch in her office and gazed out of the window. She put the phone on speaker and they both chuckled thinking about the situation.

"Yes, I totally understand. Focus on the happiness of your fiancé, the wedding planning and the restructuring of your company. The emotions of the bad stuff will take care of itself. That's what my mama always told me," Vernice said.

"You are right. Byron is the best and I couldn't have asked for a better future husband. He has been so protective, loving and caring throughout this entire process."

"Are you in the office or working from home this week?"

"Girl, I worked from both places. I was at home Tuesday and Wednesday and then came in the office Thursday and Friday. I will be leaving shortly.

The staff and Byron told me to stay home but I couldn't stay away. I want my life to return to as normal as possible. By the way, have you gotten a text or anything from Byron's rock head twin brother, Myron this week?"

"Nope, but I did have a wonderful time with him last week. I realize that Myron is different from his brother Byron. Myron's number one priority is work. He didn't say those exact words, but I read between the lines and got the hint. Over the years, I've had tons of guys not call me back for one reason or another so I'm used to it," Vernice said with a sigh.

"Listen, I have had my own self-doubts and you know firsthand. But I can truly say, when it's right, it's right. When the man wants you, he wants you bad. If he doesn't act like he wants you, always remember, that's his loss, not yours."

Vernice

"Thanks girl. I'll keep telling myself that, but there are times I think maybe I'm just not good enough for any man," Vernice said sadly.

"Alright stop right there. You are good enough. It's been more than 10 years since David, Sr. left. Stop that foolish talk. Repeat after me. It's his loss," Jillian insisted.

"I repeat, it's his loss. By the way, it's been fourteen years," Vernice corrected.

"Fourteen years! Time has flown by," Jillian exclaimed.

"Yes, it has for somethings but for love, it seems like forever. So if you can put in a good word for a sister, I would appreciate it," Vernice said.

"You know I will. I will have to tell Byron to give his brother some dating lessons because Byron is on it. He's called twice, sent a dozen roses, we spoke at lunch and he is driving down from Dayton to work here in Cincinnati this afternoon. We are meeting right after work for dinner, headed to his new office/living quarters and then wedding planning. That man is something else. Thankfully, we have the same phone service because he loves to stay connected with me and I love it. By the way, remember to keep July 4th weekend open," they both giggled.

"I wouldn't miss July 4th for anything," Vernice said.

"You are the Maid of Honor. So get ready."

"I remember and I'm honored. After you guys talk this weekend, call me and let me know what you want me to do to help. July will be here before you know it," Vernice said.

"Don't remind me. I am so excited. I'm going to let you go now because I am utilizing a temp administrative assistant this week. I am starting my company all over from scratch and want the right people in the right places," Jillian said.

Vernice

"Take care of you and don't work too hard," Vernice replied.

"You know me right. Hard work is my middle name. Love you girl and thanks for everything last week at the conference," Jillian said.

"Love you more, I had a ball with you and the entire team. Good bye," Vernice encouraged.

"Good bye, love."

Vernice pushed the end call button on her phone and whispered a prayer that God would continue to protect, guide and lead her friend.

Vernice's life was going good. She had a job, her son would soon go off to college and she was content but still alone. One day soon she hoped that she would have someone to share her life with.

Vernice finished putting her groceries away and headed upstairs with a salad and iced tea on a tray. As she put her tray down on her dresser, she repeated to herself, 'If Myron doesn't come for me,

he will miss out. It's his loss not mine.'

Chapter 2

It had been a month since she talked with Jillian. Chicago had clear and sunny skies on this April day. Vernice's goal was to get to work on time for an important meeting with an unknown client. She was walking across the Michigan Avenue Bridge headed to her office on Wacker Drive on the phone with her mom about David, Jr.'s graduation party coming up.

"Well, the cake has been ordered, his invitations are addressed, stamped and ready to send out. Just think in about five weeks, I will have a son who is a high school graduate. Yes!" said Vernice. She was focused on the conversation and not where she was walking. "Mom that sounds like a great place. Do they accept reservations? Great. Hold on so I can get a pen to write down the restaurant's number." Just as she was about to find paper, she bumped into another body.

"Oh, excuse me!" Vernice held on to her phone, but her purse flew out of her hands and the contents on the side walk. What a mess!

"Oh I am sorry, pardon me. Let me help you," Vernice didn't look at the person helping her, but realized she still had her mom on the phone. "Mom let me call you back. I just dropped my purse. I promise I will call you later today. Love you, goodbye."

Turning her attention to the stranger, "Thank you so much. I wasn't paying attention to where I was going. My purse holds everything, but my house," Vernice said as she was helping the gentleman get her belongings off of the ground.

"I don't know anything about what goes into a woman's purse. I didn't have the pleasure of having a sister, just a twin brother," he answered.

Vernice

"Well, you are lucky because women need.." Vernice stopped as she stood and saw the man's face, "Myron Randolph?"

"Vernice Washington? I didn't realize that was you." They gave each other a very awkward hug. Myron smelled wonderful and Vernice's soft perfume blended right in.

"I must sound like a babbling idiot. I am just talking away about stuff and purses," Vernice was suddenly nervous.

"That's okay. I was walking, working and not paying attention to where I was going either. That is a bad habit of mine," Myron said.

Vernice looked at Myron with no judgment, but Myron immediately felt guilty. He hadn't called her in the past month and needed to apologize. "I must apologize for not calling you. I got back from the conference and dove right into work," Myron Randolph. He suddenly remembered how her mouth felt when he kissed her a month ago. Why he hadn't called her sooner he didn't know. He was an idiot.

"No problem. I totally understand. You have been busy," Vernice took a look at the time on her phone. She put a quick hand to her hair, adjusted her light weight coat and started the timer in her head because she had exactly 15 minutes to make it on time. "So what brings you to Chicago?" Vernice said trying to sound natural. He stood about three inches taller since she was still wearing her sneakers. She wanted to ask why he would kiss her and not call her. A kiss was a kiss, but maybe it didn't mean anything to him.

"As usual, I am here on business. I am meeting with clients about something I've been working on," Myron knew he sounded corny. He really wanted to say how wonderful she looked and smelled, but didn't.

Vernice

Vernice chuckled nervously and asked, "So how long are you staying in town?"

"I am leaving late tomorrow evening for New York to another conference."

"Wow that is great. You are really on the move," Vernice replied and realized she was running out of things to say.

A little voice inside his head said, 'go for it Myron,' so he did. "Vernice, I don't know what your plans are for this evening, but would you have dinner with me? I know we both have to go, but I would love to talk to you more and not eat alone on my last night in town. Are you free about 7:30?" Myron asked.

Vernice wished she could be mad and say no, but she really wanted to go out, hear his explanation and maybe enjoy herself for once.

"Yes, here is my cell number." Vernice remembered that she gave Myron her number before, but maybe he lost it.

Myron opened his phone and he dialed the number on the card, her phone rang and then he saved it.

"Great. I will call you," Myron said as he looked directly into her eyes. He hope his eyes were saying what his mouth couldn't.

Vernice finally said, "Well, I've got to go. Hope to see you later."

"You will. I promise," Myron replied and walked quickly in the opposite direction.

Vernice ran to catch the closing elevator door to the twelfth floor. She breathed a sigh of relief because she had only five minutes to spare.

"Good morning Vernice," Raine the cheerful reception said as she entered the lobby.

"Good morning to you too Raine."

Vernice

Vernice walked swiftly down the hall to her desk, dropped off her bag and put on her pumps. Her folder with her notes was fortunately completed and on her desk. There was a note on the top of the folder, but she ignored it.

"So happy for you to join us Vernice. We hope that you had a good vacation," Charles the managing partner said.

"Thanks Charles. It's good to be back," Vernice responded breathlessly.

"Well, let me be the first to introduce you to hopefully, one of our latest clients. Mr. Myron Randolph of Randolph Technologies. Randolph Technologies began in Indianapolis but has expanded to Dayton and soon Cincinnati. After we have done our jobs, I am sure that Randolph Technologies will be global."

Everyone turned their attention toward Myron. Vernice took a deep breath, rolled her eyes and was the last to turn her attention toward him. "Thank you Charles, but that all depends on our meeting today," Myron interjected.

"Mr. Randolph, you are right, but I am confident that our team will be able to exceed your expectations. Phillip will begin the presentation and Vernice will take over at the marketing plan." Vernice nodded to Charles and looked down at the folder in front of her to see the note announcing Myron Randolph of Randolph Technologies as the new client and a 'be ready' in bold red letters. Vernice started to sweat, but had to remain calm to prove that she could deliver under pressure.

She never revealed who she worked for and what her actual job was so she couldn't be too upset with Myron for not making the connection. Vernice realized that Phillip was done and it was her turn. Vernice took her position at the opposite end of the table facing Myron who winked at her oh so slightly.

She smiled slightly to appear pleasant, but quickly became serious to focus and avoid suspicion, "Mr. Randolph, if you would turn to page twenty-four where the marketing plan begins." She gave the presentation without a hitch, stumble or slip. Myron was impressed with her and everyone at the table. When Vernice sat down, Charles Bennett said, "Mr. Randolph, what do you think?"

"I think it sounds great, but I may have a few more questions. Is it possible that I speak with...? I'm sorry, what is the young lady's name again?"

"Vernice Washington," Charles answered quickly.

"Yes, Ms. Washington. Is it possible that I may speak with you later today regarding your presentation?" Myron looked at Vernice with a slight smile. Vernice's thoughts ranged from 'what are you doing?' to 'are you crazy?'

"Sure, Mr. Randolph," Vernice said as she passed him her card with a stare that spoke volumes.

"Would you mind putting your cell number on the back just in case?" Myron added.

"No problem, there you go," Vernice said between clinched teeth. Why Myron was making a public display of her cell number when he just received it 20 minutes earlier, Vernice hoped to find out.

"Thank you," Myron replied as he put the card inside his pocket.

Vernice sat down and knew that all eyes were on her.

Charles broke the very awkward silence, "Well, do you have any more questions or requests, Mr. Randolph, for me and my staff?"

"No, I think that just about covers it. I need to double check with my team and then I will be in contact with you," Myron stood, "It was a pleasure meeting you all and hopefully we will be doing business together soon." All at the table stood until Myron left the room. Phillip slipped her a note, 'remember we don't sleep with clients."

"What was that note about Phillip?" Vernice asked once they were in the hallway and away from the others.

"I'm just saying don't sleep with him. Nobody is stupid. He might as well have asked you out," Phillip insisted.

"That's crazy!" Vernice replied.

"No it's not. How many clients have asked for your personal cell number? None, right?" Phillip pressed.

"Well, are you saying I am not attractive and no one would want my number?" Vernice asked.

"That's absurd. I have wanted to date you for a long time, but you've never given me the time of day. I don't care that you are divorced or that you have a nearly grown son. I just wanted a chance to show you that I could be your man and not just your business associate," Phillip stated.

"I appreciate the compliment, but I am not interested." Vernice knew that Phillip had dated a lot of women in the firm. She heard through the grapevine that he would wine, dine, dance and romance you until he got the "cookie." He would not be getting her "cookie." Vernice wasn't about that life of sex and no ring. She knew that the "Randolph men" believed in marriage, but she wondered if Myron could stay interested long enough to ask someone to marry him?

"Suit yourself," Phillip walked off rejected again and Vernice sat at her desk filled with unanswered questions.

"Vernice, can I see you in my office please?" Charles Bennett said as he passed her desk on the way to his office. Vernice followed him with her

Vernice

iPad and more questions running through her head.

"Please close the door," Vernice closed the door and sat down in the chair in front of his desk.

"I need for you to make Mr. Randolph happy without crossing the line, if you know what I mean. I don't have to remind you about our no 'dating the client' policy," Charles Bennett said simply.

"Well, what makes you think that Mr. Randolph is interested in dating me?" Vernice asked.

"Are you blind young lady? Clients don't normally ask for the personal cell number of a non-partner. I mean no disrespect, but it normally isn't done. I am a man and can tell what the intentions are of another man. He doesn't want to talk business, he wants you. I don't want anything to jeopardize our business dealings. Randolph Technologies is an up and coming fortune 500 tech company with the potential to be a multi-million dollar contract. Do I make myself clear?"

"Very clear."

"Unless you have a question that is all."

Vernice left Charles Bennett's office furious and excited that one visit by Myron could cause such concern.

Myron Randolph was on cloud nine as he exited the elevator on the first floor. He knew that Wallace and Bennett was the marketing firm for Randolph. Vernice being there was the icing on the cake. Myron called his brother to tell him the good news.

"Hey."

"Hello brother what's going on? How are things in Chicago?" Byron asked.

"Fine brother. Guess who works for Wallace and Bennett Marketing Firm?" Myron asked.

"Who?"

Vernice

"Vernice Washington."

"The same Vernice Washington that you are crazy about, but haven't called since we were at convention last month in Cincinnati?"

"The same. How did you know I hadn't called Vernice?"

"You forgot that my fiancé and soon to be wife is the best friend of Vernice. Have you lost your mind?" Byron pressed.

"No, I haven't lost my mind, I've just been busy," Myron said regretfully.

"Busy doing what! Too busy that you couldn't text, call, write a short email, send an instant message on Facebook, tag her on Instagram or send a pigeon! Really, man?" Byron exclaimed.

"Well, you are right I have no excuse, but I was off work for four or five days. That's a lot of work to catch up on."

"Are you really trying to let her get away again after all this time?"

"No, but did Jillian say she was dating someone? She agreed to go out with me this evening. She doesn't seem like the two timing type," Myron pondered.

"Are you listening to yourself? It doesn't matter if she is seeing someone else. You should be after her so tough that she chooses you instead of that other someone else. I've got to ask mom if she dropped you as a child. You can see what others need to do, but can't see what you need to do. This is ridiculous."

"I know and you are right. I'll find out more tonight at dinner."

"Have you called her again to confirm?"

"No, but I will as soon as I get off the phone with you."

Vernice

"Be sure to do that and don't call work first, call her first. By the way, do you know what time you are picking her up? Do you have dinner reservations or are you just taking your chances in Chicago even on a Tuesday night? It's already 1:00 p.m. my time and noon your time. Stop talking to me, call and make some reservations. Order some flowers and pay for them to be delivered today. You have money and can afford it. Do it right now. Don't ruin the Randolph reputation. That was my job and I fired myself. Text me when it is done."

"Okay, okay. I'm hanging up, now." Myron had officially been given a good talking to by his seven minute younger twin brother. He had to put his plan into action, but ignored his better judgment and called the office first. What he thought would be a quick 15 minute call turned into a four hour ordeal. It was now 4:00 p.m. in Chicago. Rush hour had begun and he hadn't even called Vernice. No flowers and no reservations.

Vernice was wrapping up her day and clearing off her desk. She got a text from Myron stating 'he was still at his hotel and would have called sooner, but got tied up. Is she still available this evening for dinner?'

Vernice replied back, 'yes, but need to get home and change first.'

Myron replied, 'fine. Text me your address and I will send a car for you around 7:30 p.m. would that be fine?'

Vernice read it and knew that it would be pushing it, but she replied to the text, 'sounds good' along with her home address. Vernice collected her things and headed out to the CTA and arrived home just past 6:30. She had a little less than an hour to become beautiful, classy and sexy. Her new black dress was perfect for this evening. At 7:25, she sat down on the couch to wait for the car to arrive. Her son David came down the stairs with an empty plate in his hands.

"Hey mom." David said.

"Hey baby," Vernice was adjusting her jewelry.

"You look nice. Where are you and grandma going tonight?" David inquired.

"Well, I am not going out with your grandmother tonight."

"Who are you going out with then?" David asked while standing at the edge of the couch.

"Look at you all in my Kool-Aid trying to find out the flavor. Do you remember Mr. Myron Randolph from Indianapolis?"

"Yes."

"Well, he is sending a car for me and we are going out for dinner," Vernice stated with a smile.

"That's cool," David said as he headed to the kitchen. Vernice turned on the TV to occupy her mind.

When he returned he said, "Well, have a good time. I am headed to the shower, homework and then to bed." David gave her a kiss and climbed the stairs.

"Night baby."

"Night, mom."

Vernice waited and waited for the car to arrive. At 8:30 p.m., a car still hadn't arrived, but her cell phone rang.

"Hello," Vernice answered reluctantly.

"Vernice, are you on your way?" Myron asked sounded excited.

"No, I am not on my way. I'm still in my living room." Vernice's answer was short because she was tired and perturbed.

"The car hasn't come yet?"

Vernice

"No."

"I am on my way to your house in a taxi," Myron said, running out the hotel lobby door.

"No, don't come now. I have work in the morning," Vernice said.

"I called a car service. I gave them your address, my credit card has been charged and they are not there? I am so embarrassed and furious. I have reservations at Bar Pastoral at 9:00 p.m."

"I've heard that place is very nice. It's too late now. I am going to bed."

"No, please. I am getting in a taxi right now. Let me explain."

"No, don't worry about it. I'm sure that you are probably leaving early in the morning so get a good night's rest. I will talk to you soon. Good night."

"But wait...," the last two words Myron said before there was no dial tone. What was he to do?

Vernice hung up the phone, turned the living room light out, headed upstairs and prayed for sleep to come quickly. She couldn't let her mind race about why Myron didn't, wouldn't and couldn't be more like his brother Byron. It had happened before and now it had happened again. Another cute dress hanging unnoticed and unappreciated back in the closet.

Dejected Myron called his brother again.

"Hello, what are you doing calling me? Aren't you on your date with Vernice?" Byron was on the couch watching a game with his arm securely around his fiancé Jillian.

"No, I'm not."

"No, you are not what?" Byron asked.

"On a date with Vernice because I blew it."

Byron raised up off the couch as he raised his voice, "How did you blow it?" Jillian was lifted out of her comfortable position and mouthed to Byron, 'what's the matter?'

Byron mouthed back, 'my crazy brother!' Jillian leaned back on the couch and rolled her eyes.

"Well, I called the office," Myron began.

"Stop right there. I told you not to call the office. I told you to handle your business and take care of the arrangements tonight with Vernice. I repeat, you were not supposed to call the office. Don't come crying to me when you are alone. I take care of what is mine and loving every minute of it. Right baby?" Putting the phone to Jillian's ear.

"You better believe it." Jillian said proudly in the phone. They both laughed simultaneously.

"So what did you do Myron?" Byron asked.

"I paid for a car to pick Vernice up and they didn't arrive. I made reservations at a very nice restaurant and nothing panned out."

"Why didn't you rent a car, put her address in your phone and go pick her up yourself? It is still early, get in a taxi and go on over to her house. Stop acting like a 14 year old, be spontaneous for once in your life."

"She said good night, hung up the phone and is probably in bed by now."

"So! Go over there and wake her up. I don't care if she has cream on her face, an ugly bathrobe on and a rag on her head. Go over there!"

"No, I am going to try again when I come back next month."

"Next month! She could be dating someone else by next month. Suit yourself. But if it were me, and I blew it with Jillian. Never mind, I am not going to blow it with Jillian. Excuse me. I am right here with Jillian." Byron's voice suddenly went silent and all Myron heard was kissing sounds in the background.

Vernice

"Goodbye brother." Myron pressed the end button on his phone.

Vernice's doorbell rang exactly one hour later. She grabbed her baseball bat. She made a quick stop to check in David, Jr.'s room and he was clearly filling the whole bed with his grown man body. She eased down the steps in the dark and turned on the light beside the front door.

"Yes, who is it?"

"It's me, Myron."

"Myron? Hold on a minute," Vernice put down the bat and took the bonnet off her head while running to the downstairs bathroom. With a quick splash of water on her face, a quick check of her hair and adjustment to her clothes, Vernice opened the door half way, "What are you doing here?"

"I just had to see you and explain. Have you had dinner yet?"

"No, I was too mad."

"Good I brought Chinese. I guess I should have checked, but do you even eat Chinese?"

"Love it," Vernice was still miffed, but gave Myron credit for coming over.

"I didn't know what to bring so I ordered half of the menu. You can keep it, let your son eat it or throw it away I don't care I just had to see you," Myron shifted his weight back and forth with eyes that pleaded with Vernice to let him in.

"Come on in." Vernice pushed the door open wide so Myron could come in because his hands were full of bags. The door shut on its own as he followed her into the kitchen. She got the plates, forks and glasses from the cabinets and placed them on the table. At the smell of food, Vernice's stomach growled. Myron opened each bag and revealed each containers contents.

"By the way, how did you get here?" Vernice asked.

Vernice

"Taxi. I will have to call one when I leave." Myron replied.

Vernice said nothing and just sat down in a chair.

Myron broke the silence as he sat down next to her, "I know that you are mad and have every right to be, but can I have your hand so we can bless this food first?"

"Sure."

"Father, thank you for this food. Help it to nourish our bodies. Thank you for this time that I have with Vernice and for her opening her door to let me in. Help me to explain myself and not have her hit me over the head with that bat at the front door. Amen."

Vernice laughed slightly and said, "Amen."

"Okay I'm nuts about you, but out of practice in relationships. It has been so long since I have been on a date that I am terrible at it. I have been focused on building Randolph Technologies with my brother. I work 60 hours a week. I eat at the office. I have a housekeeper. I travel most weeks to conferences, meetings and workshops. I only sleep at my condo in Indianapolis when I am not on the road. I really meant for us to go out earlier, but made the huge mistake of calling the office first. One thing lead to another and all hell broke loose. I did call the car company and they assured me that they were coming to this address to pick you up. Fortunately, I called back, said some not so nice words, got a refund and here I am. I am so sorry. Please forgive me."

"You are forgiven and realize that accidents and mistakes happen. I am not the greatest at relationships either, but I am a woman of my word. I like you a lot as well, but confused by so many things," Vernice said.

"Like what?"

Vernice

"You embarrassed me at my job today," Vernice said.

"How is that?"

"You asked for my cell number in front of my boss and all of my co-workers. What was that about?"

"I wanted everyone to know that I appreciated your presentation and wanted to work directly with you."

"Our company has a no dating the client policy. Your actions today raised a lot of questions and assumptions from my boss and co-workers. I was called into the office and reminded about this policy. They will be watching me very closely and I may not be able to work on your project after all."

"I'm sorry. I'll be happy to talk to Charles and explain my actions today."

"No, don't speak to Charles about any of this because he will know that we really did speak outside of the office and make it worse."

"You are right and I apologize. I have to admit that I didn't think that through."

"Right because you already had my cell number from when we met earlier on the street."

"You are right."

"On another note, you have talked about the business, your brother, long working hours and extensive travel, but what do you really want for you? You say that you are nuts about me, but you can go a month without a phone call, text, email or reaching out on social media? We had a great time together in Cincinnati, but nothing after that. I can't see how that is possible," Vernice insisted.

"I make no excuses and right now I have no answers." Myron said.

Vernice added, "Do you even want to make room in your life for another person? I am wise enough to know that some people don't want or need to be in a relationship. Your mouth says one thing and your actions clearly do something else. Since you came to me, I will lay it all out on the table for you. It's been 14 years since David's father left and I have decided that I will not settle. I did that once because you didn't pursue me. My ex-husband asked and I said yes. That was a mistake. Going forward, I want to be with someone who can't live without me, not easily forget to call and yearns to be with me every second of the day, even if he is working. There will be good and bad times, ups and downs, but I want to know that the person will have my back through it all. I want a relationship that will include a husband who wants love, hot sex filled nights, tropical vacations and to support me in all of my career pursuits. What do you think about that, sir?" Vernice asked.

"I think that is marvelous. I must confess that I have worked so much and been alone so long that I have lost sight of all of that. My brother and I agreed that we wouldn't approach a woman seriously until we were established financially, emotionally, physically and spiritually. I have all of that but still hesitate."

"Then you need to figure out how a woman will or will not fit in your life. I can't do that for you nor will I wait forever. Thank you so much for this food that will probably feed David and me for the next three days. It's late and I need to go back to bed." They both laughed lightly to ease the tension.

"Thank you so much for opening my eyes to so many things. I greatly appreciate your time and words. It's late so let me help you clean up."

"Thanks." Vernice and Myron easily cleaned up the kitchen. Myron made a quick call to the Taxi service prior to heading down the hall to the living room. The night had not met either of their expectations.

Vernice

"Thanks again for coming and the food was wonderful. You can stay as long as you like. Here is the remote until the taxi comes. Turn the bottom lock on the door as you leave and I hope to hear from you soon."

"You will. I promise you will."

"Good night."

"Good night."

Vernice climbed the stairs again and thought about the things that she said to Myron. She was proud of herself for speaking her mind and realized that the ball was in Myron's court.

Vernice heard the front door close about 30 minutes later. She went to sleep with no problem.

Myron on the other hand, didn't get any sleep that night. He got in the taxi and replayed Vernice's words. She nailed him. What woman wants to be a man's afterthought? He had to make some real changes in his life for Vernice or any woman for that matter. Taking her for granted was not going to be tolerated. Fitting her into his daily activities was a must. He couldn't just think about her when he found time. She had to become a priority in his life. If he didn't, someone else would. He was sure of it.

Chapter 3

Wednesday was a typical work day for Vernice, but not for Myron, it was a new beginning. First, he scheduled time on his electronic calendar which was synced to all of his devices each day to make contact with Vernice. Myron believed that she was in his heart, but his heart and head were not talking. The experts say that anything you do for 30 days straight is a habit and Vernice was now his new habit.

When Vernice arrived at work, there was a bouquet of roses on her desk. Myron changed his plans for the next conference and delivered the roses to her building himself and paid the person at the desk $25 to deliver them to her floor. At 9:00 a.m. he called Vernice's office and she told him how beautiful the flowers were sitting on her desk. He told her that she was more beautiful than the flowers, thanked her for last night and to have a great day. Finally, he called his brother.

"Byron, you got a minute?"

"Always for you. What's up Myron?"

"Making some changes and about to stop seeing so much of my girlfriend, 'my work' and start spending time with a physical woman and hopefully make her my wife, Vernice," Myron said.

"Now you are talking like a Randolph man. What can I do to help?"

"Well, we have got to restructure everything. Relinquish some more of my duties to other people which will include less travel and more free time."

"Exactly. Let me tell you, when there is someone to come home to and travel with, life is sweet. What do you need from me?" Byron asked.

"I need you to review an email I'm sending later. Next, we need a team retreat. Look at the calendar and see if we can get a retreat center in the middle of Indiana and Ohio for convenience. Jillian should be because you want her there and she can provide us with research and information expertise."

"True. I'll ask Diana to set it all up. There has to be a retreat center off close to I-74."

"When should we do it?" Myron asked.

"Before I get married in July. Let's shoot for two weeks which is Jillian's bridal shower and birthday. With new staff roles, we retain the roles of visionaries and facilitators rather than laborers. I think it is brilliant. So you messed up big time with Vernice didn't you?"

"Huge. She was very calm, but told me how upset she was at how I handled the situation on her job and on our first date," Myron said reluctantly.

"What did you do on her job? I thought the presentation went well?' Byron asked.

"It did, but I tried to be you instead of me. It didn't work out too well." Myron admitted.

"Remember you are the boring one. I am the suave one. You look like me but you are not me." Byron stated.

"Exactly. Vernice made it clear that she doesn't want to be any man's afterthought. She deserves to be number one, top priority and his everything." Myron said.

"She is right. No woman deserves that. What are you going to do about it?" Byron asked.

"I have been up most of the night thinking about that. I am weird and I admit it, but no longer want to be alone," Myron said sadly.

"Yes, and a geek too, but you're my brother and I love you. So, let's get her finally after 20 years!" Byron exclaimed.

"Right. Love you right back. The email is on the way and I'll call you tomorrow. Talk to you soon."

Vernice

"Bye." Byron knew that these were big steps for his brother, but he knew that Myron could do it and Vernice was worth it.

Vernice admired her beautiful roses while she ate lunch at her desk. She needed to leave on time to check up on the things for her son's graduation party.

"So who sent you flowers?" Phillip said, as he poked his head into her cubicle.

"None of ya."

"None of ya? I haven't heard that in a long time."

"Right. It is clearly none of your........... "

"I know. None of my business."

"Right." Just then Vernice's phone made the text notification sound. Phillip tried to look at her phone, but she grabbed it just in time. "Excuse you. Isn't there some place you should be?"

"Yes, I guess so." Phillip walked off just out of Vernice's view. He could hear a low laugh coming from her desk and thought, 'I will find out.' Phillip walked to the receptionist.

"Okay Raine, who sent Vernice the flowers?" Phillip asked.

"Mr. Myron Randolph why?"

"Thank you." Phillip turned and walked away thinking, 'If she doesn't want me, she definitely doesn't get to be in a relationship with one of Wallace and Bennett's biggest clients.'

Vernice received her first of many daily text messages from Myron with a picture and caption, 'this is my lunch. Let me see yours.' Vernice laughed and texted him a picture of her lunch, 'just a salad. Nothing special.'

Myron texted back, 'The salad may not be special, but you certainly are. Have a great rest of the day.'

Vernice

'You too,' Vernice smiled to herself and thought, 'wow, two messages from him in one day. I guess he is making some changes.'

Vernice called her mom on the way home from work. "Hey mom."

"Hey baby, you never called me back the other day. Everything okay?"

"Everything is okay. I got thrown off because I bumped into Myron Randolph on Tuesday. He said he wanted to take me to dinner last night, but plans got changed and he came by my house instead. We ate Chinese food and talked. This morning, I received a dozen roses and a text message at lunch from him. What do you think that means?"

"In today's terms, I think he likes you, but with you young people I can't tell. I know his brother loves Jillian. I hope that is a family trait. Speaking of

Jillian, I saw that ring online while streaming the services from the convention and it was huge!"

"Yes ma'am. It is 6 carats and gorgeous!"

"One day somebody will give you a ring that big and love you even more."

"I hope so."

"What did you call me for?"

"I called you to finish up everything about David, Jr.'s graduation party." The two had a lively conversation about the party and she almost missed her stop. She arrived home and David, Jr. was eating Chinese food leftovers. "Hey mom."

"Hey baby, how was school?"

"Fine. When did you go get Chinese?"

"I didn't. I had a friend come over last night and he brought it."

"The same guy you were supposed to go out with while you were all dressed up?"

"Exactly."

Vernice

"Well, I guess this was his apology."

"Yes."

"You going to see him again?"

"You're seventeen and still ask a lot of questions. He sent me some beautiful flowers today. Who knows?" Vernice opened her phone and showed him the picture of them.

"Those are nice. So you've got a boyfriend?"

"No, I don't have a boyfriend. Just a friend who is a boy." They both laughed and Vernice made her a plate while thinking, 'maybe one day.'

Vernice teased David, "the only boy in my life is you. You're nearly grown and not much of a boy these days."

"Oh mom. I'll always be your boy."

"You got that right." Vernice gave David, Jr. a quick hug. They finished eating, cleaned up the kitchen and said goodnight after watching some reality TV.

Vernice went to bed early and suddenly heard the bell for another text.

It was Myron again and the text included a picture. 'My current status. What's yours?' The picture showed a large pair of feet clearly under some covers.

Vernice took a picture of her feet under the covers as well and the text caption was, 'my current status as well. About to turn out the light.'

'Can I call?' Myron texted back.

'Sure.' Vernice texted back.

A 317 number appeared on her phone, Vernice answered, "hello."

"Hello beautiful how are you?"

"I am fine."

"Yes, you are."

Vernice giggled, "By the way, thank you again for the flowers. They are beautiful."

"You are welcome."

Vernice

"I have a favor to ask."

"Anything."

"Remember I told you about the firm's no fraternizing policy?"

"Yes."

"Well Phillip was hanging around my desk looking at the flowers. As much as I loved making other people jealous, don't send me anything again to work, send it to my mom's house unless it is business related."

"No problem. Would it be better if I weren't a client?"

"No, that would be worse. How was your day?" Vernice asked.

"Better now. I am in a very boring hotel in Atlanta. People tell me that this city is wonderful, but I haven't explored any of it," Myron said.

"Why don't you do some sightseeing?" Vernice asked.

"It's no fun exploring alone."

"I understand about being alone."

"You have your son and your mom."

"Yes, but he is nearly grown. He goes to school during the day, he plays sports and also works a part-time job at a small law firm in the evenings. My mom is independent and has a life of her own."

"Wow, that's great. You should be proud of your son and your mom."

"I am and would be devastated if anything were to happen to him or her."

"With everything that is going on in the world, my prayer is that it won't happen to your son or anybody else's son. When is his graduation?"

"Two weeks and the plans for the graduation party are coming along nicely."

"Do you have any plans for Memorial Day weekend?"

Vernice

"I have nothing scheduled right now. We usually just cook out and relax. Why?"

"Keep that weekend open. I may need your advice on something and include a business trip."

"A business trip where?"

"You'll see. It's late and I'm going to let you go. You have sweet dreams and a wonderful day tomorrow. Good night."

"Good night."

Sleep didn't come easy for Vernice because her mind started racing about what could be happening on Memorial Day weekend. She got out of bed and started walking from closet to closet taking inventory, being thankful and letting God know that she was ready for whatever came next.

Myron made the finishing touches on his proposal to Byron and pressed the send button on his email. He doubled checked his travel plans back to

Chicago on Friday to be with Vernice. He wanted no more delays in travel or life.

Vernice arrived to work the next day feeling good and positive about the day. She had received a morning text from Myron stating that he had a busy day, but wanted to greet her first which made her smile. The smile left when she found all of the rose buds of her flowers cut off and laying on her desk. 'Who would do such a thing?' Vernice thought. She took a picture of the scene and texted it to Myron. 'This is my current situation. The hater conference has begun. Don't send anything else to my job. Upset.' The text was sent with a sad face emoticon.

Myron texted back, 'That is awful. I am so sorry. Jealousy is horrible. I promise to make it up to you. You didn't text me your mom's address yet.'

Vernice

Vernice texted Myron her mom's address and finished it with 'bummed.'

Myron was furious and thought, 'Who would do such a thing?' He knew exactly what he must do.

Vernice was upset and on the lookout for anyone suspicious. Janice Brandice, another brand manager was coming down the hall with her heels clicking on the tiled floor. Janice had a reputation for sleeping her way onto certain projects and the Randolph Technologies Project probably was no different. Vernice realized she would have to get used to working with Janice on one project or another. Janice's long weave arrived at Vernice's desk first because she flipped her hair just as she poked her head in, "I heard you got some beautiful flowers. Did you take them home?"

"Nope they died," Vernice replied.

"After one day?"

"Yes after one day because somebody in this firm killed them."

"For real?"

"For real. Who would do such a thing?"

"I don't know."

"I don't know either but God help them if I ever found out."

"Girl, don't worry about it. From what I hear they came from a very eligible bachelor who is financially set. He won't miss the money."

"Oh really? He may not miss the money, but I really liked the flowers."

"Sorry." Janice swished her behind on down the hall.

Vernice marched to the front desk and through tightly clinched teeth asked Raine, "So you told who sent me flowers?"

Vernice

"Well just a couple of people who walked by your desk, saw the flowers and asked me who sent them."

"You can't keep your mouth shut about anything. Well, just so you know. Someone killed my flowers. They cut the tops right off and now they are in the trash. Now, go tell that."

"That's awful Vernice. I'm so sorry."

Vernice gave Raine a long stare and then turned on her heels and went back to her desk. She worked all morning in silence and left the building for lunch. She needed some fresh air, so she put on her sneakers and pounded the pavement in full stride. She could hear her phone ring loud and got to it easily on the side pocket of her purse.

"Hello."

"Hey baby. How is your day going?" It was her mom.

"Okay I guess."

"You don't sound good, but I have something that will cheer you up. Two dozen beautiful multi-colored roses were delivered here today and they have your name on it."

"From who?"

"You know exactly who. The person who put on the card, 'I hope these flowers brighten up your day like you have brightened up my life. Myron.' What have you been telling that man girl? Must be something to make him smile."

"Look at you reading my card. Thank you though. All I know is I told him the truth. It looks like he is taking my advice," Vernice smiled just thinking about it.

"What advice is that?"

"Finding room in his life for a woman. I guess it might be me."

"Go baby go! I will put them in water. Come by the house and take a look."

Vernice

"Mama, do you know how to use your camera phone to send me a picture?"

"No child. I don't. David, Jr. tried to show me once. You know I'm old and can't remember."

"Mama, you are not that old. I'll stop by tonight and take a look. I'll show you how to send a picture on your phone as well."

"Well, since you are coming over. Use your phone to text your son and tell him to come over too and yawl can eat supper with me. I don't know what yet, but I'll cook something. Love you baby and see you later."

"Thanks mom. Love you too." Vernice always felt better after talking to her mom.

Vernice spent the rest of the day getting things done and knowing she had more beautiful flowers waiting for her.

Phillip stuck his head in, "where are your flowers?"

"They died."

"So sorry to hear that."

"Are you?"

"Yes, I am, but it seems very questionable that you would get flowers from Myron Randolph when you just met him. What did you really do to deserve those flowers?"

Vernice wanted to jump up and slap his face, but knew that his connections in the company ran deep. Instead, she just gave him the worst stare with a sweet smile, "have a nice day Phillip."

Vernice turned back to her computer and found an email notification of a mandatory meeting tomorrow at 10:00 a.m. The email gave no particulars. Vernice was hopeful that this would be the announcement about the job promotion.

On her way to her mom's, Myron sent Vernice a text, 'what are your plans for the weekend?'

Vernice

She texted back, 'don't have any plans right now except the usual. What's up?'

'Flying back to Chicago in the morning. Wandering if you were free for dinner?'

'Sure. Are you really coming yourself or sending a car? Lol.'

'Lol. I deserved that. You will see. Just be ready at 7 with whatever you were going to wear on Tuesday night.'

'We'll see.'

'Yes we will. Talk to you later.'

'Later.'

Vernice walked into her mom's house and saw David, Jr.'s backpack on the floor near the couch.

"Hello, where is everybody?"

"Hey baby, we are in the kitchen.

Mama was at the stove. David was sitting on the stool just like he was when he was little. Now, his feet were on the floor, not dangling from the seat and he was reading the newspaper.

"Something smells good. How was your day David?"

"Good. Grandma tells me somebody poured a little haterade on your flowers."

"A little? To me it was a bucket of haterade. Mama tells me that I have more flowers."

"They are over there. Beautiful as ever."

Vernice saw the bouquet of roses blooming slightly from the heat in the kitchen and the water in the vase.

"Wow, they are beautiful. David, have you shown your grandmother how to take pictures on her phone?"

"Yes, but she will forget and I will have to show her again."

"Hey watch your tone young man."

Vernice

"Yes ma'am I did." David was always respectful and one of the many things she loved about her son.

"Thank you." Vernice took out her phone, snapped a picture and sent it to Myron thanking him for the flowers.

Myron texted back, 'you are welcome. Can I call you later?'

Vernice texted back, 'Sure. Eating dinner with my son and mother.'

Myron texted back, 'Tell Mother Thompson I said hello. Text me back when your feet are under the covers and that will be my sign. Lol.'

Vernice texted back, 'Will do. Until later.'

'Later.'

"Mama, Myron said to tell you hello."

"How did he say that? I didn't hear his voice on no phone?" David, Jr. and Vernice laughed.

"I just texted him the picture of the flowers and that's the message he texted back," Vernice said.

"Lord, all of this technology is making my head spin. Back in the day, we picked up the phone to see if anybody was on it. Yes, the party line and then dialed the number. Somebody answered the phone and then we talked. I could hear your voice and you could hear mine."

"I know mama, but we do it differently now. I'm hungry. What did you cook?"

"Not much. Just fried chicken, got some mixed vegetables, macaroni and cheese, rolls and I baked a peach pie for dessert."

"I love your thrown together dinners. They are always delicious to me."

"You are just happy you don't have to cook. Come on over and get you a plate. David, Jr. did you wash your hands?"

"Yes ma'am."

Vernice

"Good. Now, say grace." David, Jr. said a short meaningful grace over the food at the stove, they each fixed their plate and sat down at the table.

Vernice broke the silence at the table first. "I have two things to tell you guys. First, there is a mandatory meeting in the morning for the associate brand managers. I don't know for sure, but I believe it is about the promotion so say a prayer around 10:00 a.m. Second, Myron asked me to keep Memorial Day weekend open. What are you guys' plans?"

Her mother started, "Well, I am going with the sewing circle at church on a short 4 day cruise to Mexico."

"A cruise! That sounds nice. When did this come up?"

"When I looked at my savings and realized I could afford it. It was a package which included my plane ticket, transportation, cabin and everything. We are going to eat to our heart's content and just sit out on the deck and do nothing. I'm excited and can't wait!"

"Well, David, Jr. I've got to figure out where you can stay if I leave town."

"Oh, I was going to ask you about it later mom, but Dexter Saunders from Cincinnati asked if I was free to go to the Bahamas with him and his parents. They have a time share there and he is an only child like me and doesn't want to go alone. What do you think?"

"Well, I have to talk to his parents so give me the number. Right now, I say yes. Thank goodness I got you that passport last year. I knew this day would come and you would want to travel out of the country. How much money are you going to need?"

Vernice

"I only need spending money. Dexter's parents are paying for everything including my ticket from here to Cincinnati and then to the Bahamas."

"Wow, well, I am going to have to call and thank them."

"I'll text you his parent's number."

"Good. You got any money saved?"

"Yes ma'am about $500."

"Great, now you have a thousand. I don't want my son looking like a charity case. You may want to buy something. I do remember Dexter's mom being a little "uppity," as mama would say."

"That's an understatement if I ever heard one," Vernice's mom said.

"Thanks mom you are the greatest," David was very excited.

"Yea, yea. Finish your dinner before it gets cold." It was settled. They would all be out of town Memorial Day weekend doing something fun.

The meal was delicious and the company was exquisite, but Vernice noticed the empty chair at the table. Hopefully, one day there would be four at this table instead of three.

When they finished cleaning up the kitchen, Vernice sent Charles Bennett an email asking permission to have Friday before Memorial Day off. The email bounced back and was marked unsent. Vernice texted Charles to ask his permission which was granted and she let him know that his email had bounced back. He thanked her for telling him and that he would check with the IT department the next day. Vernice thought it was strange but ignored the uneasy feeling in her stomach as she bid her mother good night and she and David, Jr. went home.

Vernice

Vernice got in her bed, texted Myron a picture of her feet under the covers and he called immediately.

"Hello beautiful."

"Hello sir. How are you?"

"Fine now. How was your day?"

"Long and tiresome, but I'm getting better by the minute."

"Why is that?"

"Because I can hear your voice while I'm in bed."

"So, how are you again?"

"Lonely."

"The first time you are really saying it loud?"

"Yes."

"Congratulations.   You are on your way to recovery."

"Recovery from what?"

"Isolation Island." They both laughed.

"Thanks." Vernice and Myron continued talking for two hours and when she yawned, he knew he should let her go.

"Well, that's my cue. You are about to fall asleep on me."

"You are right. It's always great talking to you."

"I feel the same way. See you tomorrow."

"Until tomorrow."

"Good night."

"Good night."

Chapter 4

Vernice arrived to work early the next day. She had some things to get accomplished before the big meeting at 10:00. It was 9:50 and Vernice noticed that everyone was already in the conference room. She looked around the table and Charles Bennett wasn't there and Phillip Wallace was sitting at the head of the table collecting some mystery papers.

"Am I late?" Vernice asked nervously to anyone who would answer.

"No, you are right on time." Janice said with a smug look and slight smile. She had on a new suit, with flawless makeup and as she crossed her legs, new red bottom pumps.

Vernice's eyes fell on Bernard 'Bernie' Adams who couldn't hide anything or lie to save his life. He left an empty seat next to him and Vernice sat down.

"What's up?" She whispered.

"Please don't ask me, text me," Bernie whispered.

Vernice pulled out her phone and texted, 'Bernie what's up? Tell me. I'm going to find out any way.'

'It's bad. Really bad, but I promised I wouldn't tell,' Bernie replied.

'Don't tell just answer yes or no. Did I get the promotion?'

'No.'

'Did Janice get the promotion?'

'Yes, but worse.'

'Worse?'

'Phillip is running the firm.'

'What!? Takeover or retirement?'

'Takeover. Please don't tell that I told you.'

'Got you.'

Charles suddenly came in the conference room, "So glad that you are all here. I just have one announcement and that is all I have for this meeting. As you all know, there is an opening for Brand Manager since Lisa left and we have decided to promote Janice Brandice as Brand Manager and promote Phillip Wallace as Senior Vice President for Branding. Congratulate them both." Everyone around the table clapped unenthusiastically. Vernice's mind was racing and visions of a horrible work environment ensued. What was she to do? Would she stay and weather the storm or look for another job? She had invested so much time and effort into this company. If she left, she would have to start all over again. If she stayed, she would be miserable. Phillip wasn't a great co-worker and would be an even worse boss. Charles kept his promise and they were dismissed immediately after the announcement. Vernice went back to her desk and got a text from Myron, 'I have landed and will pick you up after work. Don't go home.'

She texted back, 'Things have changed. Meet me at my house instead.'

'What's up? You okay?'

'I will tell you tonight.'

'Sure? If you need me, call me. I will pick you up at 7. See you then.'

'See you then.'

There was a sudden uneasiness in the office. No one was talking about their weekend plans. Doors were shut. The break room was empty and everyone left the building for lunch. Vernice went to Charles' office to make sure that it was okay to leave at 4 if she worked through lunch. When she got to his office, he was not there and it was empty. She looked to see if she was in the right office, but his name plate had been removed. She went to Raine the receptionist.

"Raine, where is Charles?" Vernice whispered and Raine whispered back.

"Girl, he is gone."

"Gone where?"

Vernice

"Fired. Charles came back to his office, the door locks had been changed and the chairman of the board was waiting outside of his office along with security. He was escorted out of the building."

"I didn't hear anything."

"Charles didn't make a scene. I think he already knew that something was up."

"Unbelievable. Who is now in charge?"

"Of Branding or everything?"

"Everything?"

"Phillip is now Managing Partner. You now report to Janice and Janice reports to Phillip."

"That fast. No transition just boom, immediate."

"Yep and if you don't like it, walk."

"Wow. I guess I won't be leaving early."

"I guess you won't."

Vernice went back to her desk. She picked up her purse and phone to go for a walk to pray and meditate. She prayed, 'Lord direct, lead and guide me. God you know all about me and have the plan. Take care of this. In Jesus name. Amen.'

Vernice returned to her desk and finished her work without incident, but she realized that Wallace and Bennett would never be the same.

Myron arrived at Vernice's house at exactly 7:00 p.m. David, Jr. answered the door. "Hello Mr. Randolph. I'm David." David stuck out his hand to shake Myron's just like his mom taught him. Myron shook David's hand and realized that it was a firm handshake which was always a sign of confidence and home training.

"Nice to meet you David. I'm Myron Randolph. Is your mom here?"

"My mom's here, but not quite ready yet. You can wait here in the living room. I am headed out to the movies with my friends." Myron came in the door and took a seat on the couch. David turned and looked directly at Myron once he was seated.

"Mr. Myron? Is it okay that I call you that?"

"Yes, that's fine."

"My mom is my world. I have to leave for college in the fall and I won't be here to protect her. Please don't hurt her."

"I won't David. I can tell that you are a fine young man and it is nice to finally meet you."

"Nice to meet you too sir." A car drove up in the drive way. "I have to go now. You have a good time tonight."

"You too David."

"Thank you."

Myron got up from the couch and watched David get in the car with his friends. As they drove off, he thought, 'Vernice has done an excellent job raising him.'

Vernice called out, "David are you gone?"

"Yes, he just left," Myron called back to her.

"Hello Myron. On my way down. Just grabbing my purse," Vernice hurried just a bit to not keep Myron waiting. He stood at the bottom steps and watched as she took the steps toward him. She wore a black dress, pearls and black sling pumps. She took his breath. She was gorgeous.

"Wow, you look gorgeous," Myron whispered.

"Thank you. Let me grab my keys," Vernice got her keys off of the hook in the hallway and a wrap for her shoulders. Myron could smell her perfume as she walked past him. She was intoxicating and not just the perfume. He steadied himself and opened the front door and stood on the porch while she set the alarm and closed the door. The 'Randolph Treatment' was in full effect.

Once Myron was seated, he started the car, put on soft music and proceeded down the road to the restaurant.

Vernice

Myron broke the silence, "How was your day?"

"Not good," Vernice said.

"What happened?"

"I probably shouldn't say because you are a potential client."

"Right now, I am not a client, but a concerned friend, date and confidante. Spill it."

"You sure?"

"Positive. Shoot."

"I didn't get the promotion. The managing partner was fired and escorted out of the office by security. The grandson of the founder of the firm took his spot and a very irritating young woman is now my boss. I know for a fact that my life is about to become a living hell."

"Wow that is a lot. What do you plan on doing about it?"

"What do you mean doing about it? Nothing at this point. I need this job."

"Really? You have no plan B?"

"No. I have a son, mortgage and a car note. I have to stay with Wallace and Bennett."

"I get that, but what is your plan of action now?"

"My plan was to be promoted."

"Now that you haven't been promoted, what's next?"

"Praying a lot."

"After you pray, what are you going to do?"

"Is this a trick question?"

"No, this is a thinking question. Vernice, you have to always be thinking about the next move just in case the one you are approaching doesn't pan out. I am not trying to condemn you in any way for being responsible or someone who prays, but you should have a plan B."

"I always have been practical, proper, rational and sensible all of my life. I work hard, save my money and pay bills. I color inside the lines," Vernice stated.

"That's wonderful but think about this. What if you had no limits about money, your house and car were paid for and your son had no college money concerns? What would you love to spend your time doing?"

"My dream would be to provide marketing and promotional services to high profile clients."

"So you do have a plan B! You have thought about it, but never told anyone, right?"

"Exactly."

"Each time you thought about it you thought it was just a dream or fantasy?"

"Right."

"Why can't you have your dream Vernice?"

"My dreams usually turn into nightmares like being promoted. My son is doing very well and I'm proud of that," Vernice added.

"The young man who introduced himself and issued me a challenge tonight is already a great young man. You should be proud of him and yourself."

"Thank you. What challenge did he issue to you?" Vernice asked.

"Man to man. He told me that you were his world. He asked me not to hurt you," Myron said.

"He said that to you?"

"Yes, why are you surprised? Every mother is their son's world," Myron said.

"He's so quiet sometimes and doesn't always say what's on his mind. He says that he loves me, but has never actually told me I was 'his world' before."

"Now you know." Myron realized that Vernice didn't really know her own worth and he hoped to show her by his actions and not just words.

They road in silence with only their thoughts, the hum of the engine and smooth jazz on the radio.

Vernice

'Bar Pastoral' was packed by 8:00 p.m. on Friday evening and the volume in the room was loud. Myron checked in with the hostess.

"Vernice, you want to go outside? We have a 10 minute wait."

"Yes, please."

When they got outside, they leaned against the side of the building facing each other. Myron spoke first, "I've got a penny for your thoughts."

"My mind is racing and I don't quite know where to start."

"Start from where ever, it doesn't matter to me."

"My dad worked for the city and my mom was a teacher. They worked long hours at hard jobs to provide for me until they retired. I have the same work ethic. If the managing partner can be fired, where does that leave me? I want security with a steady pay check. Pursuing my dream is hard to think about."

"Vernice you are doing your part, but life is not fair. It's not fair how they are treating you, but you've got to be ready to fight back. You want great things for you, your son and your career. You set me straight and asked me some hard questions the other night. Now it's my turn. Are you ready to work for yourself and control your own destiny or do you want to work for someone else and let them control you?"

"I'm not a huge risk taker. Honestly, my past experiences have left me wondering if I am even good enough or have what it takes for my dream life?" Vernice stated.

Myron pushed himself off of the brick building, "First, from what I know of you right now, you are so much more than I ever thought I wanted or deserved in a woman. Second, each day we are together I want to show you and tell you just how wonderful and special you are to me. Third, how your ex-husband left you and David, Jr., I will never know. I'm just glad he did so I could have one more chance with you. I promised myself that my wife would never want for anything materially, spiritually or emotionally. More than that, I want to help her realize her dreams, go for her passions and fulfill her destiny. I want that for you Vernice." The buzzer went off in Myron's hand which was perfect timing because Vernice had no words after all that Myron had said. "The table is ready. Let's go eat some good food and talk about this another time." Myron extended his other hand toward Vernice and she gladly accepted it. He guided them through the crowd to the hostess to be led to their table. Once seated, they made small talk about everything, but her week or life decisions.

Myron surprised Vernice with two tickets to a local comedy club. Two hours of hearing Vernice laugh at a front and center reserved table made Myron glad that he got the tickets. He took Vernice back stage to meet all of the comedians, take selfies and get autographs.

"Wow that was something. Dinner, tickets to the show and then backstage passes. Thank you Myron. I had a great time." Vernice was smiling from ear to ear with no trace of her earlier despondency. He had a hand in that and it made him proud.

"I'm so glad. Randolph Technologies has the contract to do the sound for this tour so I can usually get tickets where ever they are. I enjoyed watching you enjoy the show."

Vernice laughed just thinking about all that went on. "I've never done anything like that before so thank you again."

Vernice

"We will have to do that more often. This new way of living takes some getting used to, but I'm having a great time," Myron admitted.

"Myron I can tell that you've made some radical changes in your life for me and I appreciate it."

"You are welcome and I am having a ball."

"We will have to help each other with this new living thing. Agreed?"

"Agreed."

"Do you sleep late, get up early or just go with the flow on Saturdays?"

"I am up early. Since I went out with you tonight, I am off my schedule."

"No, we can't worry about schedules when we are doing this new living thing remember?"

"Okay, you are right. What did you have in mind?" Vernice laughed.

"I thought you would be my tour guide on Michigan Avenue tomorrow around noon. What do you say?" Myron asked.

"I say yes," Vernice said with excitement.

"Great," Myron replied.

Vernice guided Myron through the streets still filled with people after 1:00 a.m. Once parked in her driveway, he turned to her and said, "Vernice, whatever you decide to do with your job, career aspirations moving forward, I support you and here for you."

Vernice had never had a man besides her father say that to her and it brought her to tears.

"I'm sorry. I didn't mean to make you cry," Myron said.

"No, it's okay. These are really tears of joy and relief. Thank you." Myron reached up and wiped a tear away with his thumb.

Vernice said, "I must look a mess."

Vernice

"No, you look beautiful as always to me," Myron held her face gently in his right hand while unbuckling his seatbelt with his left hand. Her mouth pulled at him and he couldn't resist. He went for it. The kiss was wonderful.

Myron said, "It's late, I must let you go."

Vernice leaned her head back against the headrest and said, "yes, it's way past my bed time, but just one more." Vernice came across the seat and kissed Myron without restraint exploring his mouth and lips with her tongue. Myron wasn't expecting that, but let her have her way with him and followed her lead. This was her show.

"Sorry but I couldn't help myself," Vernice said somewhat embarrassed at her actions.

"No problem at all. Glad I could help." They both laughed.

Myron found his words, "I had better let you go in the house. David might scold me again."

"Right."

Myron opened his door and came around the car to open the door for her. Walking to the front door, Vernice found her house keys.

"Well, good night and get some rest," Myron said.

"I will. Thank you again."

"You are quite welcome." Myron stood on the porch until Vernice was safely inside. He walked slowly to the car and headed to the hotel.

Vernice headed up the stairs, quickly undressed and was asleep five minutes after her head hit the pillow.

Myron, on the other hand, was going to be awake for a minute. He called the only person he knew that he could awaken at this hour.

"What's up brother?"

"You alone."

Vernice

"Yes. Jillian stayed at her place tonight only because I have a meeting early in the morning and didn't want to disturb her. I can't wait to be married. I'm sorry, but my ADD just kicked in at the mention of her name. What time is it any way?"

"It's almost 3:00 a.m. your time."

"What's wrong? You okay?"

"Yep, I'm fine. I just had a great time with Vernice."

"That's great! So things are progressing."

"Yes they are. Thank you very much."

"So what's the problem?"

"There really isn't a problem and that's the problem."

"Stop stressing and relax. You are feeling her, she is feeling you so enjoy yourself for once."

"You are right. I am giving her the Randolph treatment just like dad taught us. Her son also gave me a warning tonight."

"Really? What did he say?"

"His mom is his world and don't hurt her."

"Good for him. He always was a good little boy. Now, he is becoming a great young man. You or I would be doing the same thing if it were our mom."

"Right."

"So, what's the problem?"

"Nothing. She's got some work stuff going on and I want to support her with that. I'm just trying to balance it all. It is hard trying to make sure that I give her the attention that she needs without letting work suffer."

"I realize that work has been your wife, girlfriend and first love. Now it is time to tell that girlfriend that you have somebody new. This is what we've been working for and promised ourselves. The women we have chosen are independent and our money is not their priority but our time, care and love. We've got to be sure that we enjoy them."

"You are the smartest brother I have."

"Of course, the only brother you have. You are smart too, but just not as smart as me." They both laughed. Byron continued, "So what's the plan?"

"I will be back in town on Sunday night. Can we meet on Monday to begin putting into action the plan I emailed you?"

"Yep, I'll be there. Let's meet at 10:00 a.m. because we are staying in Dayton this weekend and driving in Monday morning. Are you staying the whole weekend in Chicago?"

"Yes, I am going to do some sightseeing tomorrow afternoon, dinner, live jazz tomorrow night and then church with her on Sunday."

"Sounds like a plan. Okay, I am going back to sleep. Love you brother."

"Love you right back. Good night." Myron always felt better after talking things out with his brother. Byron was the best at getting his head back on track. Myron felt much better as he arrived back at the hotel, unlocked his room door and finally put himself in bed for the next few hours. Sleep came easily for him as well.

Chapter 5

David, Jr. woke up with no smell of bacon, eggs or biscuits coming from the kitchen. He thought he heard his mother come in late last night or early this morning, but why was she still in bed? David eased down the stairs and just as his nose indicated, his mom was not in the kitchen cooking anything. He ran up the stairs as fast as he could and knocked on his mom's door. "Mom are you okay?"

"Yep, I'm fine just sleepy. Open the door David I'm descent."

"What happened? No bacon, no eggs and no biscuits. You alright? What happened last night?" David asked.

"Look at you all up in my Kool-Aid and don't know the flavor. Mr. Myron took me to dinner, a comedy show and then drove me home."

"Wow, you at a comedy show?"

107

"Yes, I went to a comedy show."

"Well, alright mom," David said with a big smile.

"Thank you very much. Myron told me that you gave him a warning on your way out."

"And?"

"And nothing. He thought that was great and so did I. I knew you loved me, but didn't know I was your world."

"Yes, mom, you are my world."

"I'll take that. Let me get my robe on and make some breakfast."

"Yes!" David ran down the steps and started preparing his usual breakfast cereal concoction of *Wheaties*, *Captain Krunch* and *Frosted Flakes*. When Vernice arrived in the kitchen, she smiled but made a 'yuck' sound while looking at the concoction. "I don't know how you eat all of that sugar."

"Love it mom, love it."

Vernice

"What's your plan for the day?"

"Well, I have practice at 1. Why?"

"Myron is supposed to pick me up around noon. Are you hanging out at the house, grandmas or going out with friends this evening?"

"I am going to be at the house playing games with some friends online and will order a pizza. Are you going to be gone all day?"

"Don't know that, but probably. Did you need something?"

"No, I just wanted to know when I should set your curfew."

"Boy! I'm your mama, a grown woman and don't need a curfew."

"Yes, you do. You need to get your beauty rest."

"What are you trying to say?" The phone rang and she could tell that it was her mother. "Hey mama, what's going on?"

"Hey baby, nothing just called to check on you guys this early morning."

"We're fine. Let me put you on speaker phone 'cuz I'm cooking. What's up?"

"Well, if I was hungry, I'd come over, but I went to the district women's prayer breakfast this morning. Guess who was there?"

"Who?"

"Ida Mae Washington."

"Really. The last I heard she lived in Florida."

"She does, but she came to Chicago to stay with her daughter because she had knee surgery and somebody needs to keep her kids."

"So what was she talking about?"

"Your ex-husband and how much he is doing in LA."

"Great," Vernice said sarcastically.

"I told her how fantastic my daughter and grandson are doing too."

"What did she think about that?" Vernice asked.

Vernice

"She was only slightly amused." Vernice's mom said.

"She hasn't seen David since he was 2 years old."

"I don't want to see her now," David yelled in the background. "I am grown and don't need none of them."

"David don't be like that," his grandmother said. "Good or bad they are still your family. They may not be good family, but they are still your family. If you needed a kidney, we might have to contact them for a match."

"I understand grandma, but I don't need a kidney, thank you very much." David had a right to be irritated and didn't want to hear anything about them. "Mom, I'm headed back to my room. Call me when breakfast is ready."

"Okay, baby." Vernice watched as David left the kitchen with his cereal and climbed the stairs.

"Mom, I think we upset him talking about the Washingtons."

"I can tell, but he is going to have to face it one day."

"Yep, but not today. You didn't tell them anything about the graduation party?"

"Lord, no. I don't want those people all up in nothing we are doing. I am sorry, but I just had to brag on you both. She told me about her no good son, I was going to tell her about my wonderful daughter and grandson."

"No problem mama."

"Are you seeing Brother Myron anytime this weekend?"

"Well, we went out last night and he is supposed to call around noon. I'll let you know how it goes. Let me finish breakfast and check on David."

"Okay, bye baby."

"Bye, mama."

Vernice

Vernice hurried to finish the breakfast and called David downstairs.

"Go ahead and have a seat. Say grace please."

"Thank you God for the food we are about to receive. Help it to nourish our bodies and serve you in spirit and in truth. Amen."

"Amen. So tell me what's bothering you."

"I'm sorry, but all of that talk about people who don't care enough to call or see me since I was two is disturbing me. Where have they been? What could have kept them away from me? After I was four years old, I didn't see my dad again. Gone? Why? I know what you told me mom, but why?" David pleaded.

"Baby, I am sorry that our conversation upset you. I was a little upset with your grandma for even telling your other grandmother anything about you or me. On the other hand, we can't control what other people do, only ourselves. I don't want this to take anything away from your graduation next week. We are going to have a good time celebrating your achievement, you will have fun in the Bahamas and when you come back, we will get you ready to go to college. You hear me?"

"Yes, ma'am. I hear you, but it still hurts."

"Exactly. Nobody is asking you not to feel the hurt. I am asking you to not let the hurt stop you from anything in your life. They don't deserve that much influence. You have worked too hard to let this get you down. Let's eat."

Vernice and David ate while they watched the Saturday morning cartoons, ESPN sports and anything else on television to take their mind off things. A sudden ding on her phone made her stop to view her text. "Early, he's coming early? I'm not ready."

"Don't panic mom, I got this. Go get ready."

"Thanks, you are the best."

Vernice

"I know." Vernice flung the towel at him teasingly as she left the kitchen.

Myron rang the doorbell and David answered, "Good morning Mr. Myron. Mom is upstairs getting dressed she should be down in a minute. Come on in."

"Great."

"By the way, are you a gamer?"

"Sure, what's the game? I'm rusty and haven't played in a while." David showed Myron the box with *Marvel vs. Capcom* on it.

"I love anything Marvel. I had the comic books too," Myron said.

David loaded the game and it was on. Vernice realized that Myron was here when she heard two voices downstairs. She got dressed and didn't know where they were going, but jeans was what she felt like wearing. Vernice came out of her bedroom and stopped at the top of the stairs to listen to their conversation. It was apparent that David was winning, but Myron was hanging in there. A hot tear ran down her cheek. She always wanted David to have a father figure in his life. It was an answer to prayer to have Myron in her life now. She wiped the tear, blotted her face with powder and went downstairs. "Who is winning?"

"David of course. I am so out of practice."

"You're okay Mr. Myron. Just need to play more often."

"Yes, I guess you are right. Ready Vernice?"

"Yes, I am. David, if your plans change let me know."

"They won't mom."

"Okay, see you later. Text me when you are back in the house. I love you."

"Yes mom. I love you too. "

"Bye David." Myron said as he closed the front door behind Vernice.

Vernice

"Bye." David said with a sigh. David liked his mom going out with Mr. Myron. He only wanted his mom to be happy and if Mr. Myron did that, more power to them.

Myron opened the car door for Vernice and once they were both settled, Myron proceeded to Michigan Avenue.

"How are you doing today?" Myron asked.

"I am doing fine. I slept late today so I am doing very well."

"Good. Sorry I kept you out so late."

"No problem it was worth it."

"Well, Michigan Avenue has been on my 'to do' list for some time. I thought we'd catch the sights, look in the windows and then have dinner some place nice."

"I didn't dress for someplace nice."

"Don't worry we'll improvise," Myron said.

At the Art Institute of Chicago, Myron took her hand and they took their time looking into each window, observing the people, smelling the food and passing the time of day. With no agenda, it was a luxury for both Myron and Vernice. They purchased popcorn from *Garrett's*, sneakers from the *Nike Store* for David's graduation gift and one of the latest gadgets from *Crate & Barrel*. Vernice suggested that they go over to State Street where 'the real people' on a budget shop.

Myron asked, "So you naturally stay on a budget?"

"Yes, sir. I have to. I have no help from David's father. My mom used to babysit David, Jr. when he was younger so I have watched every penny that I've made and spent."

"I am the more frugal, not cheap brother, between us."

"You sound like you are apologizing for watching your money."

Vernice

"Maybe but I want it to be clear that I'm not cheap. I don't particularly like cheap people."

"Why is that?" Vernice asked.

"Because my parents taught us that cheap people are usually cheap in all areas of their life including love, affection and attention to others."

"Well, I never thought of it that way. I agree that you are not cheap. I can tell by your clothes and electronics. So is the theory the same with selfish people?"

"Probably so. I don't particularly like selfish people either. Do you?"

"No. Love and everything that comes with it should be given freely and in large quantities."

"I agree." Myron was making mental notes of all that was and wasn't said.

When they arrived at *Filene's Basement*, they agreed to go their separate ways and meet at the front of the store. Myron didn't shop so he didn't spent much time in the Men's section. Vernice found a cute red dress, a pair of low heeled sling back pumps, both on the clearance and headed to the cashier. Her hoop earrings and bracelet complemented her new dress along with the makeup already in her purse.

When Vernice finished checking out, she found Myron standing at the entrance with a small bag in his hand.

"Did you find everything?" Myron asked. Vernice smiled knowing that Myron wasn't much of a shopper and 'ready to go.'

"Yep, I found everything just fine. Look at you all patient and waiting."

"Thank you ma'am. I know patience is required for any man with a woman and you are well worth the wait."

"You think?"

Vernice

"I know it."

"Thank you." Vernice smiled at Myron and lightly punched him on the arm as they headed down the store escalator. Myron checked his phone and realized that they had been walking, talking and taking in the sights for at least three hours.

"I made reservations for 5:30 so we should head back to my hotel to change for dinner."

"Sounds good." Vernice's mind started racing, 'his hotel for what? Calm down. Change clothes dummy and go to dinner.' Vernice knew that Myron wasn't about to do anything that she wasn't willing to do. David texted that he was home so she relaxed and looked forward to the rest of the evening.

Myron put his room key in the door and turned to Vernice, "Are you okay?"

"Yes and no."

"Relax. My room is clean. You can go in the bathroom and take all of the time that you need. It's just me. Okay?"

"I'm know I'm acting like I am fifteen instead of forty."

"No, you are just nervous and beautiful." They both laughed and Myron held the door for Vernice. When she entered, he pointed her in the direction of the bathroom. "Go ahead."

She heard the television come on and realized that it was CNN first and then ESPN. She was thankful that she had shaved her legs and applied moisturizer. Nothing worse than 'being ashy' as her mother called it. There was mouth wash for her breath and she freshened her makeup. When she opened the door, Myron was sitting on the bed watching television.

Vernice

He stood to not make her more nervous, "You are gorgeous as usual." He wanted to touch her, but resisted.

"Thank you." Vernice moved far away from the bed to sit in the chair at the desk.

"I'll be out in a minute." Myron smiled as he closed the bathroom door with a different shirt in one hand and a pair of slacks on the hanger in the other. He thought, 'she is so nervous and that is a good sign. Thank you Lord.'

Vernice hadn't been alone with a man in a hotel room since her honeymoon with David's father. Sure she had been on dates, but nothing close to this.

"Ready?" Myron asked Vernice coming out of the bathroom bringing her back to the present.

"Yes, I am."

"Leave your things here. We'll get them when we come back."

Vernice got her purse and off they went. The restaurant was on the 95th Floor of the *John Hancock building*. She had been told about the awesome view and delicious food. Today, she would find out for herself. They were seated at a table with a full view of the Lake.

"I haven't taken time off from work on the weekends in about ten years and to be with you makes it wonderful."

"You really know how to make a girl feel good."

"That's my goal." They both laughed.

"I must say that I was really moved by you playing that video game with David."

"Really?"

"Yes."

"I enjoyed it and realized how much I hadn't played. I am not addicted to video games, but Byron and I played a lot when we were teenagers. That's why we're both into technology."

Vernice

"I remember people calling you the 'church boy' nerds," Vernice said.

"Yep and Byron would punch somebody right in the eye for that and that's why he got so many whippings at home, school and the conventions. My brother is still the fighter between us," Myron mused.

"You aren't a fighter?"

"Not by nature but I'm learning how. I'm a hard worker but know that I have to fight for what I want especially in relationships," Myron looked directly into Vernice's eyes and continued, "You don't deserve the left overs of me. I want to treat you so well that you can't live without me."

Myron's statement took Vernice's breath away and the assistant waiter arrived just in time with their drinks. Vernice took a long drink of sweet tea and said, "Myron you deserve a woman who will be by your side through thick and thin and be that lap for your head to lay in."

"I'm hoping that I am looking at her."

"I hope so too." Her eyes never straying from his. Myron leaned in to seal it with a soft kiss and Vernice didn't resist. The salads arrived and their conversation turned to the view, shopping and the sights of the day.

It was 7:30 p.m. when they left the restaurant and Myron had one more surprise.

"Do you like jazz?"

"Love it."

"Boney James is at *Andy's Jazz Club*. You up for it?"

"Really? Love to." Vernice thought, 'thank God for lower, comfortable heels.'

At the club, Myron gave his name at the door and they were escorted to a reserved table near the stage for the second night in a row. The show started on time and the music was incredible. The

Vernice

Club didn't have much of a dance floor, but there was an area right next to their table. Myron was a preacher's kid, nerd with two left feet, but he wanted Vernice in his arms to sway to the music. He whispered in her ear, "Can I have this dance?"

"Sure, but where?"

"Right here." Myron and Vernice fit in each other's arms like a hand in glove. Boney James pointed them out to the audience. Myron could see that Vernice was tired from the day so after two more songs they left the show. He told her to wait in the hotel lobby while he retrieved her bag. The bed was there, it was convenient and his body was screaming.

Myron opened the door to leave and stopped because Vernice was standing in front of him. His heart almost stopped beating. He still held the door open with one hand with his key and her bag in the other.

"I've never done this before, but I have not made love in fourteen years. Do you know what that feels like?" Vernice asked quietly.

Myron was stunned and shook his head 'no.'

"Can I come in and show you exactly what I mean?"

"Yes," Myron whispered. His brain was not functioning properly. He took two steps away from the door and Vernice crossed the threshold into utter darkness. Myron followed behind her and the door closed on its own. Myron's back was to the door and he made no movement to turn on a light because he forgot where the light was. Feeling like a 16-year-old idiot, he waited on Vernice to make the next move. He knew that Vernice was presenting herself to him so she was in charge. Vernice turned toward him and placed her body on his and gave him the kiss of a lifetime. He dropped the bag and key in his hands to take her in his arms. She dropped her purse on the floor and her mouth found his ear. She said, "Make love to me."

Myron thought he dreamed those words or his mind was playing tricks on him. He knew he wasn't dreaming because when he kissed her this time, her response was worth it all. There was no music or TV, the sounds of pleasure made its own music in perfect harmony.

Hours later still wrapped in each other's arms, Vernice's phone rang.

"Hold on baby, let me get the light," Myron said while caressing her shoulder.

Vernice rolled over slightly to pat down her hair because it must be a complete mess. When Myron found the light she found his shirt to put on and continued to look for her phone still ringing in her purse. Her dress and one shoe was on the dresser and the other shoe was in the desk chair.

'Oh what a night,' were the first words that came to Vernice's mind. She blushed from head to toe knowing she had never made love like that before, but hopefully would again and again.

"Hello," Vernice said after finally finding her phone. She sat down on the bed while Myron adjusted the covers for her to be back in his arms.

"Mom? You Okay?" David, Jr. asked.

"Yes baby I'm fine." Vernice said reluctantly.

"Where are you?" David, Jr. pressed.

"With Mr. Myron," Vernice confessed.

"This late? I mean this early? It's 5:00 a.m. I got up to go to the bathroom and knocked on your door and you weren't there. You coming home or do you want me to go to church with grandma?"

"Nope, I'm coming home to explain everything and take you to church," Vernice said.

"Mom, you don't have to explain anything to me. I was just a little worried. Take your time."

Vernice

"Listen at you all grown up," Vernice smiled and looked up at Myron who smiled and winked back.

"Mom, I am not a kid. I totally understand that adults who care about each other do adult things. That's fine with me," David Jr. reassured Vernice.

"Give me an hour or so and I should be home. I'm fine. Bye son," Vernice laughed as she hung up the phone.

"Everything alright?" Myron asked quietly in her ear trying to gauge any sign of regret, guilt or shame. Myron wanted nothing more than to take a shower together, make love until noon and then order room service, but right now that wasn't to be.

"Yes, I'm more than alright. I am fantastic," Vernice said happily.

"I don't want you to have any regrets."

"Not one. Last night was terrific," Vernice purred.

"Well, as much as I would love to stay in bed with you all day, we've got to go and face the world," Myron said.

"In time, but right now I want to lay here one more hour and see what happens," Vernice said seductively.

"Gladly," Myron quickly obliged.

Two hours later, Myron got up, found the hotel robes and let Vernice access the bathroom first. Myron turned on the TV to keep him company until she was done. In his mind, Myron knew that last night sealed the deal for him. He must marry her as soon as possible. He didn't have much experience with women as his brother, but Vernice was everything that he wanted and more.

"Your turn," Vernice said as she exited the bathroom.

Vernice

"Thanks," Myron said and gave her a warm kiss. Vernice gathered her things, waited patiently and knew that their relationship was altered forever.

On the way to her house, the Boney James channel on Pandora serenaded them and Myron broke the silence. "I know that this is a little late to ask but is there any possibility that you could get pregnant?"

"Nope, there is not," Vernice said quietly.

"Why are you so sure? I didn't plan to make love so we didn't use protection." Myron asked.

"I had a hysterectomy thirteen years ago right before David's father left. He was careless and I was only able to have one child," Vernice said looking out the truck window.

"I'm sorry," Myron said as he turned toward Vernice.

"It's not your fault. I would have never approached you last night without telling you about a pregnancy or any other problem. You are too good of a man for that, but know this, I would have loved to have had your child, Myron," Vernice insisted.

"I would have loved that too," Myron said as he gently squeezed her hand.

As Myron turned into the driveway, Vernice said, "I don't know how David, Jr. is going to take this but let me start the conversation, okay?"

"That's fine with me but I am not ashamed of anything that we did last night," Myron insisted.

"Yeah but I'm David, Jr.'s mother," Vernice added.

"You are right. I could be in trouble again. He did warn me," Myron said and Vernice giggled.

Myron and Vernice walked to the door hand in hand. David, Jr. was sitting on the couch watching TV and waiting on their return.

"Good morning David."

"Good morning mom. Hello Mr. Myron. You guys ready to go to church?"

Vernice

"No I think we need to talk first," Vernice said.

"What about?"

"About last night."

"What about last night?

"I have always been very honest with you David and don't intend to lie. Mr. Myron and I slept together last night. How do you feel about that?" Vernice inquired. Myron stood by and waited for David, Jr.'s response.

"I feel fine. I have already told Mr. Myron that I don't want him to hurt you. He says that he won't and I believe him. I know that you are an adult. You have needs and that is fine with me. You are still my mom and I worry. It scared me when you weren't in your room, but I trust Mr. Myron," David said.

"Thank you David. I value your trust greatly," Myron said relieved.

"You are right David I should have called. If there is a next time, I will call," Vernice reassured David, Jr.

"By the way you look mom, there will be a next time," David, Jr. smile.

"Boy!" Vernice blushed.

They all laughed and Vernice headed upstairs to change. Myron and David, Jr. began playing the video game to take the awkwardness out of the moment. Vernice returned in only a few minutes and they rode together to church.

Myron dropped Vernice and David, Jr. at the church entrance and parked the car.

Just as Vernice and David, Jr. were seated in their pew, in walks Ms. Ida Mae Washington. "Hello Vernice," Ms. Ida Mae said.

"Hello Ms. Washington," Vernice responded cordially with no regard to their history.

Vernice

"Is that my grandson David, Jr. all grown up? Wow, he's handsome like his father," David said nothing, nodded slightly and just stared at his estranged grandmother.

Myron walked up and said, "Excuse me. Hello Ms. Washington."

Myron sat down on the pew next to Vernice and David, Jr.

"Well, aren't you one of Bishop Randolph's sons?" Ms. Ida Mae asked.

"Yes, ma'am. I'm Myron."

"Of course you are. Your brother is the real trouble maker. What are you doing here this morning?" Ms. Ida Mae asked.

"I'm here on business and thought I would come to church with Vernice and David. By the way, my brother's name is Byron."

"Oh, how are your parents and your brother?"

"They are all fine. Thanks for asking." Before Ms. Washington could ask any more questions, service started with music and the choir singing. Vernice's mom turned in her seat and rolled her eyes at Vernice when Ms. Washington sat on her same pew.

After the choir sang, they clasped hands to pray and opened their phones for the scripture. The church announcements were next and David, Jr. stood when his graduation invitation was read. There was thunderous applause and both grandmothers yelled out, "That's my grandson. That's my grandson too."

Everyone laughed, but David, Jr. wanted to crawl under the seat. "Oh mom no they didn't."

"Sorry, but yes they did," Vernice said trying to comfort him.

Vernice

Myron smiled and told David, Jr. "Don't worry David. I've had worse things happen to me in church. Congratulations though."

"Thank you." David, Jr. rolled his eyes again. Myron and Vernice just smiled. The announcer also mentioned to the audience that the out of town guests were Myron Randolph and Ms. Ida Mae Washington. During the fellowship time, people shook hands and greeted the guests warmly. Single women crossed the aisles to especially speak to Myron. They shook his hand, hugged him real tight and made small talk about his plans while in town. Myron replied, "I am leaving in the morning and I do have plans for the evening." A few women looked Vernice up and down, rolled their eyes and walked away. One young woman put a piece of paper in Myron's front breast pocket as she hugged him. He retrieved the paper and gave it right back to her. She slid it inside her bra and said, "Your loss." Vernice and David's Jr.'s mouth dropped open.

Myron turned to David, "See I told you about things happening in church."

"Wow," was all David, Jr. could say.

When service ended, they had dinner at Vernice's house complete with the family pack of *Harold's Chicken* with Vernice's side dishes. It was finally four people at Vernice's table. Throughout the meal, they laughed, talked and joked about the happenings at church including the loud grandmothers. Myron and David, Jr. put their plates in the sink and retreated to the living room to play their now favorite video game. Vernice and her mom continued cleaning up the rest of the kitchen and Vernice's mother whispered, "Well how did it go last night?"

Vernice

"Great. I had a wonderful time. I bought a cute new dress and shoes from Filene's basement because he took me to the top of the *John Hancock* building to the 95th floor. Oh mom, it was so high and the city was beautiful from up there."

"Really? Way up there? You didn't get sick?" Her mom asked.

"Nope, not at all. I was fine."

"That is great. What else did you do? 'Cuz David, Jr. called me at midnight and said you weren't home yet."

"What? David, Jr. called you?"

"Yep. Don't get off the subject young lady."

"We just went to hear some jazz at *Andy's Jazz Club* and he brought me home. What did you and David, Jr. talk about?"

"I talked to him about his father's family, etc. I said that I was sorry if I upset him on Saturday and he was going to have to face it one day," she said.

"You and Ms. Washington making a scene today didn't help. Myron on the other hand, helped lessen the blow," Vernice added.

"Myron has been a great addition to this family hasn't he? In the living room with David playing that video thang or whatever. That's great," Vernice's mom said.

"Yep, it is. I cried hearing them on Saturday playing that game. I always wanted that for David, Jr. I didn't have many men in the house because you warned me about that," Vernice recalled.

"Sure did and it was a good thing. Myron is a Randolph. He comes from good stock and that makes a difference. It took him long enough to get here though, but he's here now."

"According to our conversation last night, he plans to stay," Vernice said.

"What did he say?" her mom asked.

Vernice

"He said he was going to contact me every day and come every week until I couldn't live without him," Vernice said with smile.

"Woohoo! I love a man with a plan. Hallelujah!" Vernice's mom did a little dance in the middle of the kitchen just like at church.

"Mom, shh. By the way, you move pretty well for a spry older lady."

"Hush up 'chile. You are only as old as you feel."

"Right." They laughed again and continued cleaning up the kitchen. Vernice conveniently did not tell her mother all that happened on Saturday evening. She wasn't ready for a scolding just yet. David, Jr. was fine and that was all that mattered. Vernice and her mom went into the living room to watch Myron and David, Jr. play for a while. The game ended and so did their time together. David, Jr. won again. He was still the champion and always would be in Vernice's eyes. He said goodnight to his grandmother and turned to Myron before leaving, "Mr. Myron will you be back in town next weekend?"

"I plan on it. Why so you can beat me again?" Myron teased.

"Yes and could you come to my graduation and after party next Saturday?"

"Love to." They gave each other a fist pump and David, Jr. retreated to his room. Vernice's mom looked at Vernice and winked. Vernice winked back while blinking back tears.

"Well, I've got to go too. An old lady's got to get in the house before the street light is on. I know that Jim Crow is over, but I am still black and it is still Chicago." Vernice's mom got hugs from Vernice and Myron along with a plate of leftovers for dinner the next day.

"Call me when you get in the house mom."

"I will 'chile. I will."

Vernice

Myron sat on the couch and watched Vernice looking out the window until her mom drove down the street. She sat beside Myron.

"David, Jr. beat me to the punch."

"About what?"

"Asking if you could come to his graduation and graduation party on Saturday."

"It is an honor to be asked especially by him. I should be in town on Friday and stay the weekend again. Listen, about Memorial Day Weekend. I know you were coming to Cincinnati for Jillian's bridal shower, but can you take that Friday off and come to our company's retreat with me?"

"I guess. Mom and David are both going out of town.

"That's great. How were you travelling to Cincinnati for the shower?"

"I was going to drive."

"Nope, this is now a business trip so I am going to have our administrator Diana get you a plane ticket."

"A plane ticket? Why? What kind of business?"

"We'll talk about that later."

"What about Wallace?" Vernice asked.

"Don't worry about that. For now, I want to see you that weekend and don't want you on the road alone. I'll pick you up at the airport and give you more of the Randolph treatment."

"Oh yeah?"

"Yes ma'am."

"Oh wow. Sounds great." Vernice's phone rang which let her know that her mom was home safely. At the end of the call, Vernice turned back to Myron and he said, "Now where were we?"

"I was hoping you were about to do this," Vernice leaned in and they kissed with a passion that could have led to part 2 of last evening, but David, Jr. was right upstairs so it would have to wait for another time. Myron finally released her and gave her one more kiss at the door.

"Good bye beautiful. Until next time,"

"I look forward to it."

Vernice waved to Myron as he drove off.

When Myron got back to the hotel, he texted a picture of his feet under the covers and Vernice did the same. Myron called to hear her voice once more.

"Hello gorgeous."

"Hey handsome."

"Oh wow, I could get used to that,"

"I hope so,"

"I know it's late, but I'm missing you. I now know what is attached to those feet under the covers and it is making me want you even more," Myron said.

"Me too," Vernice giggled.

"I have to go. There is a cold shower with my name on it. Good night."

Vernice continued to laugh and said, "Good night."

She turned over in her bed and cried tears of joy.

Chapter 6

The next day Vernice arrived to work to find that her desk, computer, person effects and work files had been moved to a small cramped space near the supply closet. They sent weak Bernie to tell her that her office was needed for a new branding associate. To add further insult, she would train and report to the new brand associate. Vernice thought, 'How do I train someone to do my job and be my boss?' The handwriting was on the wall. Vernice had been praying, but now it was time to put the prayers into action.

Just as he promised, Myron texted three times a day and called in the morning and at bed time. He sent pictures of a sandwich, flowers or a selfie. She was his habit and he had no intention of breaking it. She didn't tell him what was going because she wanted to talk to him in person, hold him again, kiss him for eternity and hear him say that he had her back. Her father said that 'women have at least 10,000 words a day to say.' Vernice felt like she had about 50,000 words to say and none of them were good about this company.

It was Friday and Myron arrived early so he leaned against the passenger door of the rental car to wait for Vernice. He texted her that he was outside so 'Don't get on the CTA, I'm here.' Vernice's heart leaped in her chest. At 5:00 p.m., she literally ran out the front door and into Myron's arms. He had to catch her so they wouldn't fall from the force of her embrace. "Hey baby, what's the matter?"

"Too much. Get me out of here. Please."

Myron opened the door and secured her before closing it. "Where to?"

"Let's go to my house first. I need to change, get David and head to the restaurant to make final arrangements for the graduation party." They

Vernice

drove in silence for a minute just listening to music until Vernice could collect herself.

"I am so sorry, but I have been so angry all week that I haven't been able to think straight."

"What happened?"

"I came in Monday morning…………." Vernice began, but Myron interrupted her.

"Stop right there, Monday morning and you are just now telling me on Friday? Babe, I have been in touch with you at least three times a day since Monday and you mentioned nothing."

"I know, but I wanted to wait until you were here and tell you in person. I didn't want you to worry or be upset and interfere with something you had going on this week."

"I thank you and appreciate the concern, but that's not good. Seeing you is great, but the stressed look on your face really worries me. I just have one thing to say. Don't do it again. I know that you are independent, but you don't have to go through anything else alone again. I love you and if it affects you, it affects me."

"Go back, go back, you what me?"

"I love you. I've known it for a long time."

Vernice unbuckled her seatbelt, came across the console and kissed him thoroughly while the car was stopped. The cars behind them honked their horns because of the delay.

"I wish you had told me that sooner. I think I've loved you since Convention, but thought you didn't want me when you didn't call. I've got to stop being afraid to tell you anything. I promise from now on. Okay?" Vernice said.

Myron pulled the car in a parking lot to get out of the flow and anger of traffic. Vernice fit in his lap and her arms were around his neck kissing him with no restrictions.

Vernice

When she finally released him, Myron said, "Okay. I agree I am much happier with you in my arms. Do you want to tell me the summary of it now or wait until we get to your house?" They both laughed and Vernice kissed him again before continuing.

"I'll tell you the abbreviated version now. I went into the office on Monday. My desk, computer and personal effects were moved to a small cubicle far away from the other associate branding managers. Long story short, they are trying to make me train someone else to replace me or make me mad enough to quit. I've asked myself all week, what do I want?" Vernice said.

"What did you decide?" Myron asked patiently.

"I really want my dream of my own marketing and promotion firm."

"You don't want to stay and fight?"

"No, I have invested a lot, but I believe it is time to move on."

"Alright, what does it take to have your own marketing firm?"

"I don't know, but I'm about to find out soon."

"Once you find out. I believe that Randolph could be your first client once I tell my brother. Your first opportunity to impress the team will be the retreat during Memorial Day Weekend. After that, who knows?"

"For real? Thank you Myron, I won't let you down." Vernice's face now had a huge smile and she breathed a sigh of relief.

"I know you won't. That's the smile I love that lights up my life. Now, get off my lap before I won't stop you and let's go have some fun planning this party for your son." She did just that with a giggle. Vernice was so glad for Myron's support.

Vernice decided not to change clothes, but called David to come out of the house to get in the truck. David, Jr. was smiling when he saw Myron in the driver's seat. David got in and said, "Mr. Myron you came!"

"I did just as I promised."

"Good to see you."

"Great to see you too." Vernice wiped another tear.

Once at the restaurant, the manager showed them to the private dining room. A big sign, graduation caps everywhere, balloons and the cake would make the room and the event perfect.

While Vernice was finalizing details with the restaurant manager, David, Jr. walked over to Myron who was watching Vernice intently.

"Mr. Myron I can tell that you really like my mom."

"No, David, I'm in love with your mother."

"Why didn't you marry my mom instead of my dad?"

"I wanted everything to be perfect. I wanted my education, career, money in the bank, a house, a car and then a wife. Because I waited, your dad married her first."

"He hurt her real bad.

"Yes, and he hurt you real bad too. You are a great guy and I would be so proud if you were my son."

"Thanks. I don't think that you will hurt my mom."

"I am going to do everything in my power not to."

"Thanks." David, Jr. walked away satisfied with his answer. It seemed when Myron showed up he made his mom smile. David didn't know him very well, but he knew that he could keep a promise.

The next day, Myron arrived at Vernice's house at 9 a.m. sharp. He smiled while watching her in action. David was due to the auditorium by 10, the ceremony started at noon and the graduation party started at 3. Everything worked perfectly. Myron went inside to save their seats in the auditorium while Vernice stood at the entrance waiting on her mother. At 10:30, Vernice' mom and Ms. Bonita, from her mom's sewing circle, came walking in the entrance.

"Mom, here we are," Vernice said as they approached.

"Hey baby, everything okay?" Vernice's mom asked.

"Yep, everything is fine. David is lining up, Myron is inside and everything is already at the restaurant."

"Girl, you got you some good help this time didn't you baby," Vernice's mom said.

"Mama you are a mess. Great help is what I would call it. Hello Ms. Bonita," Vernice said with a smile.

"Hello Vernice. I heard about what's going on from Frances. I come to see for myself. I saw ya'll Sunday looking like a cute little family."

"Not quite, but thank you so much."

Myron stood to let the ladies into the row of saved seats. At exactly noon, the processional music began and 455 students marched in with white, gold and red robes on down the aisles to their seats on the stage. David, Jr. walked right by them nervously and he waved. He was proud of his family that now included Mr. Myron. He saw his mom wipe her eyes. The graduation ended at 1:30 with time to take pictures with David, Jr.'s friends and teachers.

They arrived at the restaurant at 2:30 and the guests began arriving at 2:45. Vernice had two girlfriends from church assist as hostesses.

David, Jr. was busy taking selfies when a man walked into the room. Vernice recognized him immediately. He was older with gray hair, wrinkles on his face and dressed in designer clothing. It was him, David Washington, Sr. Myron was standing nearby and he heard her say, "Why is he here?"

"Why is who here?" Myron asked hearing the concern in her voice and seeing her body tense.

"David's father," Vernice said quietly.

"He's here in the room right now?" Myron asked.

"Yes, he is walking directly toward David, Jr."

Vernice and Myron walked quickly toward them.

"Congratulations son!" David, Sr. was loud and left nothing to the imagination. The music was still heard but the DJ had turned down the sound.

"Who are you?" David, Jr. asked.

"I am your father. I am David Washington, Sr. Your grandmother told me that you were graduating today," David's father replied.

"How did you get here?" Vernice asked.

"I followed you guys here after the graduation ceremony," David, Sr. answered.

"You didn't see me graduate?" David, Jr. asked.

"No because I didn't have a ticket," David, Sr. was looking directly at David, Jr.

"Why are you here?" Vernice said angrily.

"I wanted to tell my son congratulations," David, Sr. said still smiling.

"Congratulations? When you left 14 years ago, you told me that you wanted nothing to do with me or our son. Why now? Why today?" Vernice pressed.

"I just wanted to tell him congratulations and that I am proud of him," David, Sr. answered.

"Well, you have said it. Now go," David, Jr. said boldly.

"Go! I'm not going anywhere," David, Sr. exclaimed.

"Yes, you are. You are making me and my mom uncomfortable. I don't want you here at my party. You haven't bothered to be in my life, paid child support or sent a birthday card in fourteen years and you show up today. Mr. Myron has showed me more interest in the past three weeks than you have my whole life. Please leave!" David, Jr. yelled.

"Who is Mr. Myron?" David, Sr. yelled even louder attempting to embarrass David, Jr. and Vernice.

"I am," Myron replied firmly.

"I remember you. You are one of them Randolph boys aren't you?" David, Sr. said with a slight chuckle.

"She always did have a crush on you until I came along," David Sr. said.

"It doesn't matter about the past. I am here now and I suggest that you leave. It's apparent that Vernice nor David want you here. Leave on your own or I will help you to leave," Myron threatened.

"Is that a threat?" David, Sr. asked sarcastically.

"No, that is a promise." Myron said emphatically.

"Who and what army is going to make me leave?" David, Sr. shouted.

"The Chicago Police Department is going to make you leave sir. This is a private party and you are not welcomed," one officer said as two officers entered the room.

"I am this boy's father, it's his graduation party and I have every right to stay even more than this man here," David, Sr. said boldly.

"Well, according to this arrest warrant, you only have the right to remain silent, anything you say may be used against you in a court of law...." The officer continued to read David Washington, Sr. his rights as the other officer handcuffed him and removed him from the room. Ms. Ida Mae Washington entered the room and said, "I didn't mean to disturb David, Jr.'s party, but I knew that this would be one way to get him to town and captured. He's been selling drugs and racketeering all over the country for years. With as much as he has done, you won't ever be seeing him again."

Vernice

"I hate to say this, but thank you Ms. Washington." Vernice replied amidst anger, fear, embarrassment and relief that they would finally be rid of David Washington, Sr.

Ms. Washington turned toward David, Jr. as she said, "I realize that this is hard for you, but as your grandmother, congratulations David. Your dad has done some horrible things, but wants you to live a life opposite of his."

She then turned to Vernice and said, "Vernice you have done an excellent job with David, Jr. Keep moving forward and enjoy your life. Myron take good care of them both."

"I will," Myron replied standing very close to Vernice and David, Jr.

"Are you going to stay a little longer?" David, Jr. asked Ms. Washington.

"No, I can't stay. I have a plane to catch."

"Can I at least get a picture?" David, Jr. asked his grandmother.

Ms. Washington wiped a tear and said, "of course, baby."

Myron took a picture of Ms. Washington, David, Ms. Frances, Ms. Bonita and Vernice. The rest of the party went off without incident. When Ms. Washington left, David, Jr. turned to Myron and said, "Thanks Mr. Myron for standing up for me and my mom."

"No problem David. This is your day and I didn't want anything to spoil it. If you or your mom would have wanted him to stay, I would have dealt with it, but it was clear that you both wanted him to go," Myron said.

"Peanut, come and take our picture," David asked with a smile. Peanut was David's friend from elementary school who took a picture of the three of them and Vernice cried again.

Vernice

The rest of weekend was spent at Vernice's house with much laughter, food and fun. David, Jr. beat Myron once again at the video game. Vernice's mom went home so happy for her family that she thought her heart would burst. It was getting harder for Myron to leave Vernice, but he knew that he would see her again in a week. Every time Vernice thought about it all, she just cried more tears of joy.

Julia A. Royston

Chapter 7

Sometimes isolation can be a good thing. Vernice's desk was so far away from everyone that she spent her time preparing and planning her next move. She visited the information management staff who provided her with the public history and documents about the firm. Vernice arranged to meet with Charles Bennett to get his advice about her situation. Charles proved to be a wealth of information and offered his assistance in any way. He was now working as a consultant and spent a lot of time on the golf course for business and pleasure. He encouraged her to use her time wisely and not to get caught off guard by the new firm's traitorous leadership. She organized her online files, physical folders and any notes that she had collected over the years.

In the evenings, she went home, ate quickly with David, Jr. and worked on her business plan. She drafted a logo, letterhead, social media banners and mapped out her marketing strategy for Thompson Media Group. Myron texted Vernice every day and she told him about her progress. He offered suggestions or resources to keep her moving in the right direction. She realized she now had a partner in life that actually wanted to see her do well and realize her dreams.

The upcoming weekend would involve getting everybody ready to leave town. Friday night Myron came in town and they all stayed in to watch movies with huge bowls of buttery popcorn that Vernice insisted could only be done right on the stove. Saturday was a day of shopping and packing along with a quick visit to Vernice's mom's house to help her pack. Myron and David watched TV in the living room and frequently smiled at each other while listening to the conversation upstairs.

Vernice

"Baby, I only need a change of underwear each day and one dress. Nothing special," Vernice's mom said.

"Mom, you have to have more clothes than that. My mama will not look like the homeless woman on this cruise. Let me pack for you," Vernice teased. Her mom smiled, sat down in a nearby chair, smiled and watched as Vernice repacked her bag.

"Thanks baby, I greatly appreciate it," secretly, Ms. Frances wanted to spend time with Vernice before she left town. Ms. Frances knew with the status of Vernice and Myron's relationship, she would be seeing very little of her daughter soon. Ms. Frances was thankful that Myron had the means, love and character that her baby needed to live that happy life that she so desired.

At the airport with tissue in hand, Vernice kissed and hugged both of the loves of her life. As always, tears flowed and she said a prayer, 'keep them both safe. I love them so much.' Miraculously, they were on the same plane and Vernice got a text when they landed. Parting ways at the *Northern Kentucky/Greater Cincinnati Airport* David, Jr. joined the Sanders family and Myron headed to his Cincinnati office to meet and stay with his brother. "See you later David. If you need anything, you have my cell," Myron said to David, Jr. as they left the baggage claim area with their bags and one final fist pump.

"Yes, sir. I will text you later." David, Jr. said as Myron watched David, Jr. walk away with the Sanders and their son, Dexter. Myron realized that he couldn't love him more if he were his own son. Myron arrived at the Cincinnati office right before noon.

Vernice

"Good to see you brother." Byron stated as he hugged his brother. He was glad to see Myron and even happier to see the huge smile on his face.

"You too."

"How are things in the windy city?"

"Warm, calm and loving. Having the time of my life. Her son is wonderful too."

"That is great."

"Had a little drama with his biological father last weekend, but the Chicago police came, arrested him and the calm returned."

"Wow. Sounds like a television drama. You okay?"

"Yes, we are all fine. You and Jillian have had enough police drama for the both of us for a long time."

"You've got that right. So what is your current status on things?"

"I love her. She says that she loves me too. I'm going to ask her to marry me. I don't know exactly when and what ring to buy so I might need your help."

"When do you want to ask her?"

"Yesterday, but I don't want to overshadow any of your plans, the shower or wedding in anyway. It is about you and Jillian right now."

"No, it's just not about me and Jillian. It's about you and Vernice as well."

"Don't worry, we haven't really discussed it. She is coming here on Friday and not leaving until Tuesday. I hope we have time to sit down and talk about it. I think I might need Jillian to find out what size, shape, etc. she likes."

"Hold on." Byron picked up his phone and touched one button.

"Hey baby. What's up?" Jillian said answering on the first ring.

"Always you. You doing okay?" Byron asked.

Vernice

"I'm fine what's going on?" Jillian inquired realizing that they had just talked about two hours ago.

"I've got Myron here." Byron said.

"Hey Myron!" Jillian exclaimed.

"Hey Jillian."

"Jillian baby, Myron is going to ask Vernice to marry him," Byron announced.

"Yes, yes, yes! Yippee! I am so excited! This is so great. Congratulations! Can I call her? Can I tell her?" Jillian asked.

"NO!! You can't tell her. I called you to find out Vernice's preference for a ring style, size and color. Myron needs to know," Byron and Myron both laughed at Jillian's exuberance.

"I'm sorry. I know I can't tell her. I can't wait. How soon do you want me to ask her or call her or you know what I mean?" Jillian stammered.

"Were you this excited at our engagement?" Byron teased.

"Of course I was! I was super excited. I was even more shocked than excited. I couldn't believe that you loved me and wanted to marry me. You know I love you right?" Jillian giggled.

"I love you more and can't wait to see you later," Byron said in his low sexy tone.

"Okay, okay you two. Back to my request. I need to know the details before this weekend. She will be here on Friday." Myron said.

"I got you. I will text her this evening and let you know," Jillian said.

"Baby, we're still meeting after work, right?" Byron said.

"Yes, my place or yours?" Jillian asked.

"I think Myron is going to stay at my place so I will meet you at your place around 7," Byron said.

"Do I need to have dinner ready?" Jillian asked.

"No, you just be ready because I am bringing dinner," Byron said.

Vernice

"Yes, sir," Jillian giggled.

"Okay, bye baby. Love you," Byron said.

"Love you too. Bye Myron and congratulations. Talk to you later."

"Thanks Jillian. Man, you've got it bad for that woman. I'm so proud of you," Myron said.

"Yes, very bad and in the old days we'd said, takes one to know one." They both laughed giving each other a fist pump.

"You usually only chase this hard after technology ideas. What's up?" Byron asked.

"Technology doesn't feel this good in my arms or kiss this well," Myron replied.

"Get down brother! That's what I'm talking about. So what's next?" Byron exclaimed while smiling from ear to ear.

"She's got a horrible situation at her job. I just think with the way our lives work that we both need wives that have a job/career/business that is mobile and not tied to an office building. With the right Executive Administrator, Jillian can be mobile and go on a cruise with you any time she wants to right?" Myron asked.

"Right. So what's your point?"

"I am done with Wallace & Bennett as our potential ad agency. Vernice is doing research to start her own firm/consulting business. What do you think?"

"I think it is great and I know you want to help her, but she is just starting out. On the other hand, she could be a consultant on our team and/or be a liaison to another firm until she gets her connections built up. Is this a test run this weekend?"

"Yes. She was to be the lead at Wallace & Bennett if we had contracted with them. She's good or they wouldn't have had her make the presentation. Since then, they've had a hostile takeover and they are trying to boot her out because she didn't play footsie with him figuratively and horizontally."

"Got it. Since Jillian will be there too, she might be interested in throwing some business Vernice's way."

"That sounds great. Vernice had a meeting with one of her former partners and he could throw some business her way. She has low overhead, saved her money and if she married me, she'd be set."

"You mean when she marries you?"

"Right."

"Let's do it. We do need to revisit the legalities of the company with future wives and in your case, a step-son and how that all would work."

"Call Boris and set up a meeting. The sooner the better. There are a lot of changes to be made. Let's go!"

"We better call our parents too. Have you talked to mom and dad lately?"

"Nope." Byron dialed the number and their parents were thrilled with the news about the addition of a daughter-in-law and a grandson. The brothers were feeling real good about the direction of their company and love lives.

Vernice's phone rang just moments after she dropped her mom off.

"Hello."

"Hey Vernice, how are you?" Jillian asked.

"I'm fine girl. How's everything going with you?" Vernice asked.

"Busy trying to get it all done. I hear that we are going to be roommates this weekend?" Jillian teased.

"Yes girl and I can't wait to get out of this city," Vernice sighed.

Vernice

"Why what's been going on?"

"A little bit of everything. First, my love life is going great! Myron, Hallelujah! Prayers answered. I love him. He's caring, loving and gentle. David really likes him. That is great. On the other hand, work is nuts. The founder's grandson took over as managing partner in a hostile taken over."

"What? Girl, that's crazy."

"Girl, there's more. I came in two days ago and they moved all of my personal things to a back area, near the janitor closet and clearly, away from all of the other brand managers."

"No!"

"Yes but Myron has been encouraging me to think about going into business for myself. He wants me to pursue the idea of having my own marketing firm. I don't know about it all and it makes me nervous, but I have been doing my research and it is doable."

"Go for it! What's stopping you?"

"Me! I'm stopping me."

"What do you need to get started?"

"First, clients. I have some money saved. You know I've always been frugal. David has a full ride to Ohio State in the fall."

"Wonderful! So what's the problem?"

"I've always been a 9 to 5 job person. Punch the clock, do what I am told, keep my head down and get a check."

"Again what's the problem?"

"What if I fail? What if I don't have what it takes? What if I'm not good enough?"

"Okay, stop right there. I think that is remnants of your ex-husband talking, but your new man says you can do it. Believe in yourself. I confess that Byron makes me think outside the box too. I may need your help. Let me be your second client. I am quite sure that Randolph Technologies will be your first." They both laughed at the idea.

"Well, I have been talking to the former partner and he may have some leads on clients for me as well. We can talk this weekend about some problems you have and some ideas that I have."

"That is fantastic. Okay, I am not good at beating around the bush so I'm going to give it to you straight."

"What?"

"You know Myron's going to ask you to marry him right?"

"Well, I guess so, but that is left up to him."

"Right, but you are my girl, so I want to make sure that the ring is right. So what type of cut of ring do you like? Is it emerald, oval, square, one stone, many stones. What?"

"Jillian, I only had a plain gold band with David's father. We didn't have much money and we couldn't really afford a big ring. So I don't know."

"Time to shop! We will have a little time on Friday morning to head out to *Tiffany's* and see what you like! Yes! I'm excited!"

"*Tiffany's*! Girl are you kidding me? Those prices in *Tiffany's* are crazy!"

"You are not buying it. He is. We need your ring size, shape and color. I'm so excited I could scream."

"Girl, you are so crazy! Just think, if he asks me, we'll be sisters in law! That's even crazier."

"No girl, it is when he asks and not IF he asks. According to Byron, he is in love with you big time. I think I'm going to cry. I have always loved you like my sister."

"Same here, Jillian. Same here."

Vernice

"Look how God is working this out!" The two women stopped to dry tears and catch their breath because prayers were answered and dreams were coming true.

"Girl, gotta go, almost to work. Love you and we shall talk soon."

"Love you more. See you on Friday."

Vernice arrived in the office just five minutes before 9:00 a.m. She logged into her computer and there was an urgent email that stated that a company policy had changed. 'We must change the professional look of our office. No personal pictures, notes, dolls, slogans or posters that are not specifically company, brand or client related on or around your desks or office spaces. Boxes are located in the break room and your personal effects should be removed upon your departure this evening and not on Friday. Signed, Phillip Bennett, Managing Partner.'

Vernice got up from her desk, headed toward the break room and on her way heard voices in a nearby office.

The one person said, "I've got the picture right here. We have what we need to nail her."

The other voice in that same room said, "Yeah, but I want her to quit. If I fire her, she can collect unemployment. I won't do anything until after the holiday. I love to see people come back from a holiday and get bad news."

Vernice froze in her tracks and thought, 'that's horrible!' She heard them coming so she went into a nearby cubicle to see who came out of that office. It was the new girl and of course, Phillip. She grabbed an empty folder off of a desk and walked right by them. They didn't speak or acknowledge her presence. Vernice went into the break room, got an empty box and went back to her desk.

She texted Myron, 'are you busy during lunch?'

He texted back, 'no but are you okay?'

Vernice texted back, 'Yes. Call you at noon.'

He texted, 'okay.'

Vernice called Myron and told him everything that happened that morning. Her next call was to her lawyer.

When she returned to the office twenty minutes later, Raine whispered with her head still down, "Psst. Watch your back. They are coming for you."

"Who?" Vernice asked as she slightly hesitated prior to walking away.

"Top dog." Raine replied.

"Got it," Vernice answered. Sometimes it pays to associate with the big mouth in the company. Vernice drove her car to work so she could take her box home in her car and not on the CTA.

It was amazing to Vernice that it seemed that God was closing the door for her. If one door closes, another door will open. Surprisingly, Vernice was at peace about it all. She kept working until the end of the day. With her purse on her shoulder and the box in two hands, she looked back to a clean desk and thought, 'bring it on God.'

Chapter 8

The next three work days were a repeat of Monday. There were more changes in her work load and schedule so it gave Vernice even more reason to leave the firm. Phillip called her in his office at 3:00 p.m. on Thursday afternoon.

"Hello Vernice, have a seat." Vernice didn't recognize the office because it had been remodeled since Charles Wallace's exit. Vernice was seated in a chair that looked like it should be for a child compared to the very large chair and desk that filled over half of the office.

"I have decided to remove you from all of your current projects at the end of the day today. I want you to return to your desk and take all of your client folders to Janice and she will redistribute the assignments."

"So, what do you want me to do after that?"

"Research."

"Research? Isn't that the junior associate's job or the information services department's job?"

"No, it is now your job. You will do all of the research for the branding department."

"Are you kidding me?"

"No, I am not kidding and if you don't do it, you can just quit."

There it was, right out there. She had been warned and now it was actually said. A stillness came over her and she said, "No, I will do what's best for the company."

"Great. Close the door on your way out." Vernice was dismissed. Vernice went back to her desk, collected all of her folders and reported to Janice. Janice smiled when she saw Vernice coming, "Hello. Have a seat. I have to make this call and I will be right with you." Janice got on the phone with whoever and talked for a solid hour. Vernice sat there, waited and decided that this weekend she would launch *Thompson Media Group*. It was 4:30 p.m. and she would be leaving the office at 5:00 p.m. At exactly, 4:45, Janice ended the call and asked Vernice, "Why are you here?"

"I was told by Phillip to bring all of my working files to you," Vernice said.

"Sit them there and leave. Thanks." Vernice placed them on the small conference table and exited. She was so mad she could spit. In spite of it all, she remained calm, professional and poised. With the strength of God, encouragement of Myron and help from her friends, Vernice now knew she had something else to do and somewhere else to go. As Vernice exited the elevator to leave the building, she said, 'Hello to my new life.'

Friday morning Vernice caught the 6:00 a.m. flight from Chicago and was in Cincinnati by 8:00 a.m. Vernice stepped off the plane in Cincinnati and practically ran to baggage claim. She just wanted to see, touch and kiss the man that had been texting her all week, calling her at night and loving her from afar. When she got to baggage claim, he was there with that smooth caramel skin, jeans that hung just right, a polo shirt, sneakers and a dozen roses of every color in the rainbow. No words. No hello. No pretense. She dropped her purse at his feet, put two arms around his neck and kissed him like he was the last man on earth. He kissed her back like he was dying of thirst. Her red suitcase went around the carousel alone several times.

"Hey baby with a greeting like that, I may not let you get back on that plane. It is great to see you too."

"I didn't mean to embarrass you, but it's been a rough week. I just needed to be in your arms and feel like there was somebody with me in this whole mess."

Vernice

"First, I'm not embarrassed, but overjoyed. Second, I love you, you got me now and always baby. Finally, are you hungry?"

"Starving."

"For me or food."

"Both."

"Oh yeah, that's what I like to hear." They both laughed in each other's mouths as they kissed again. She picked up her purse, he handed her the flowers while he retrieved her bag from the carousel.

Myron took Vernice to a quaint European styled restaurant serving all types of delicacies in the over the Rhine area of Cincinnati.

"That was wonderful," Vernice said, "love the crepes."

"Glad you liked it. Since I've been working here this week, I've been getting breakfast here most days alone because I don't cook and you know that Byron is with Jillian."

"Of course. So, what's the plan for the day?" Vernice asked.

"First, I am going to take you to Jillian's office. She said that you guys are going to spend some time together this morning. Byron and I have a meeting with our lawyer in an hour or so. Jillian is going to bring you back and then we will head up to the retreat site."

"Sounds great. I just wanted to say thank you."

"What for?"

"Being you, all of your support and love."

"You are welcome. We are just beginning. It goes up from here." He kissed her sweetly, paid for the check and dropped her off at Jillian's office.

"Can I help you?" The receptionist asked Vernice.

Vernice

"Yes, Vernice Washington to see Ms. Jillian Forrester."

"Right this way Ms. Washington. Ms. Forrester has been expecting you." The receptionist knocked on the door, "Ms. Forrester, Ms. Washington is here."

"Show her in. Thanks Jessica." Jillian jumped up out of her chair and ran to the door. The two hugged so tight and the tears flowed.

"I am so happy that you are here. I can't tell you how glad I am to see you," Jillian said.

"Girl, I am glad to be here. I feel like I should pinch myself already."

"Why? You deserve it. Myron giving you the Randolph royal treatment?"

"Yes, girl. He picked me up at the airport looking like something on the cover of GQ magazine, had a dozen of multi-color roses in his hands and a big 'ole smile."

"That's the way God works. He will blow your mind if you trust Him."

"You're right about it. I don't want to get in your way so I'm going to sit right here and be quiet."

"No, you are not disturbing me. It is Friday before a holiday. I am wrapping up things so I don't have to come back after our little outing to the jewelry store. Let me give you a quick tour and then we can chit chat about where I see the company headed." Vernice and Jillian had been friends for years, but this was the first time that Vernice had actually toured Forrester. The building was state of the art, security was tight and the technology was revolutionary. They returned to Jillian's office and discussed her vision.

"So what do you think?" Jillian asked.

"I think it is awesome. Yes, you need to expand your client base and I have some ideas on how best to do that. Let me go over my notes and put a proposal together. Review it, let me know what you think and then we'll proceed from there."

"Sounds good to me." Jillian's phone rang. "Guess who?" Jillian asked Vernice who was smiling from ear to ear.

"Byron," Vernice answered.

"Right," Jillian put the phone on speaker, "Hey babe what's up?"

"Nothing much what's up with you guys. Vernice doing okay? Myron is about to die over here." Everybody laughed.

Vernice chimed in, "Hey Myron. I am fine baby. Jillian's giving me the royal treatment. I'm in good hands."

"Just checking to make sure. You can't be too careful with my precious lady over there."

"Woohoo, go ahead Mr. Myron. Lay it on thick," Jillian teased.

"I mean to. It's been a long time coming, but a change has come," Myron announced.

"Preach brother," Byron yelled.

"Yippee!" Jillian yelled. They all laughed.

"Hey, we are about to go into our meeting now and should be done by 2. You ladies want to come here and hang out until we are ready to go?" Byron asked.

"Sure. Are you guys going to eat lunch or are we going to get something on the way out?" Jillian asked.

"Eat on the way up. Let's try *the Inn* off of I-74. I'll have Beverly make reservations. I just don't want to be held up in traffic," Byron said.

Everyone was all smiles as they said goodbye.

Vernice and Jillian walked in the front door of the jewelry store and Vernice whispered, "Girl, you do all of the talking. I don't have a clue what I am doing in here."

"I do, so follow my lead."

They were quickly greeted by the young woman who had helped Jillian when she came to pick out her engagement ring.

"Hello Ms. Forrester, how are you?"

"I am fine Amy, how are you?"

"I'm great. Are you here to pick out your wedding band?"

"No, my fiancé is going to take care of that. I am here to help my best friend look through some engagement rings to see what she likes. A little birdie has told me that she might be getting engaged soon so I need to help the bird tell the man what to buy," laughter all around. Jillian continued, "Just like me she doesn't have a particular shape, size or setting that she knows that she wants so she needs the full treatment."

"Great. Let's get started," Amy said.

There were rings of all sizes, shapes, colors, yellow gold, white gold and platinum. The selection was amazing. Jillian texted Myron, 'Vernice's ring size is a 6 and a half. Do you have a price range?'

'Nope. I just want to buy what she loves.'

'Great. More to come.'

'Thanks. You are the best sister in law."

'I am the only sister in law. Lol.'

'Lol. Right.'

Vernice asked, "Jillian what do you think?"

"Oh no, this is all about you. I want to know which ring you love."

"I love this one how much is it?

"Ma'am, let's see what it looks like on you," Amy said.

"I know that you want me to fall in love with it and then tell me the price. I get it." Vernice said with a chuckle. The ring was gorgeous and when the

Vernice

light hit the ring it bounced off of the walls in the entire room. With her long slim fingers, the ring fit like a glove because it was her size.

"Ma'am that ring is $14,300 with the band set."

"Lord that is a car not a ring! Get that off of my hand. I'd be too scared to wear it. It is way too expensive. Can I see something much smaller? I just couldn't think of Myron spending that much on a ring."

"Okay, no problem, but I must say it looked great on you," replied Amy.

Vernice breathed a sigh of relief when the ring was safely back in the case. Jillian could tell that nothing jumped out at Vernice quite like that first ring. Jillian knew that she loved it and texted Myron the size, price and designer of the ring. It was all set. Jillian loved helping make someone else happy. Vernice asked a passing sales associate, "Where is the restroom?"

"Right this way ma'am," the other sales associate informed. As soon as Vernice walked away, Jillian turned to Amy.

"Alright Amy, I am the little birdie. It is a surprise. I have texted her boyfriend about that first ring, size and everything. He will be coming sometime today to buy it. He is my fiancé's twin brother. He looks just like Byron Randolph, but his name is Myron Randolph."

"Great. I'll be on the lookout. Here she comes." Amy whispered.

Jillian said to Vernice, "Girl, we have been in here over an hour and a half. You ready to go?"

"Yes, I am if you are?" Vernice answered.

"Thanks so much for your time," Jillian said as she gave Amy a quick wink.

"No problem, Ms. Forrester. Congratulations to you both. Have a great day."

Vernice

At Randolph Technologies, they were greeted by Beverly, the administrative assistant who quickly escorted them to an open, versatile and multi-use area of the office. All areas of the office could be seen and flowed from one place to the other. The design was incredible. Vernice and Jillian could see Byron shaking hands and saying goodbye to a gentleman. He gave Jillian a big smile and wink while walking toward his work area to stack some papers neatly inside his credenza. Vernice got a text from David, Jr. who was having a great time at the Sanders' house and would leave on Sunday for their trip. Byron came into the conference room and embraced Jillian. He kissed her and she asked while their lips were still close, "He gone to get the ring?"

"Yep."

"Wonderful." The kiss resumed.

"Um excuse me?" Vernice asked. "Could someone tell me where Myron Randolph is?" Byron and Jillian smiled, ending the kiss, but still embraced.

Byron said, "He had to run an errand and the way he drives, he won't be long. How was your flight Vernice?"

"It was fine. I haven't flown much, but it seems to agree with me," Vernice said as she smiled just thinking about seeing Myron again.

"That's good to know because my brother and I love to travel." Byron said.

"Vernice it will be fine girl. I love to travel too so I have a sneaking suspicion that we will be double dating a lot," Jillian added.

"Looks like it," Vernice agreed.

"I don't know about you both, but I am hungry. I am going to get the bags and start packing the car. Where are you parked babe?" Byron asked.

"Right beside you," Jillian said.

Vernice

"That's where I always want you," Byron said with another wink grabbing Jillian's hand to lead them to the living quarter's entrance.

"Is he a constant flirt?" Vernice asked.

"Yes girl, 24/7 and I love it," Jillian said seductively. Byron laughed as he held the door open for them both to the newly built living quarters complete with a four car garage, four bedrooms, five bathrooms, living room, dining room, kitchen, small sauna, theatre room and enclosed patio. It was more spacious than Jillian's condo and very secure as well. Byron was obsessed with keeping Jillian safe. He wouldn't move in or allow Jillian to visit until the security system was set-up.

When Vernice asked about all of the security, Byron answered, "I don't want anything to happen to my love."

Jillian and Vernice waited in the kitchen until everything was settled in the car. When the women opened the truck back doors, the garage door suddenly went up. Myron pulled his car in the open space. "Hey everybody!" Myron was thrilled and smiling from ear to ear.

"You're back!" Vernice exclaimed. Vernice ran around the car to greet him. Byron and Jillian were arm and arm, smiling while watching the exchange between Myron and Vernice. "Yes baby, I'm back. Excuse me a minute." Myron embraced Vernice and gave her a long luscious kiss. "Sorry had to get that out before our ride up. Hello Jillian."

"Hello, Myron. Glad to see you happy."

"Glad to see it myself."

"Let's go, I am hungry and I hate traffic," Byron announced. When Myron was seated up front, he removed the box from his pocket and quickly opened it for Byron to see. Byron mouthed to his brother, 'wow.' Myron put the box in the glove compartment, Jillian said a prayer and they were off for the first of many double dates.

The Inn was a working farm located about 40 miles outside of Cincinnati with a porch that surrounded the house. It was once a restaurant, but now a bed and breakfast. The barn was converted into a gift shop and there was an additional restaurant built that could seat up to 250 people. The conversation was lively and the food was delicious. After dinner, they only had 20 more miles until the retreat site in an adjacent town. They checked into their rooms and agreed to meet by the bonfire pit which was complete with rocking chairs, wood benches and God's earth for their view.

Myron gathered four long sticks, the ladies had blankets for cuddling and Byron brought out his stash of chocolate, marshmallows and graham crackers for s'mores.

They were all having a wonderful time but Vernice seemed uneasy.

"You okay?" Myron asked Vernice.

"I'm fine just happy," Vernice said.

"That's what I like to hear," Myron said.

"It's okay to shed a few tears girl you are among friends," Jillian added.

"Yesterday, I was so worried about my job and how things were going to turn out. Right now, I am not worried about anything just enjoying everything," Vernice said.

"Tomorrow is not promised. Live it up," Byron said.

"Right," Vernice agreed. The fire was warm, relaxing and bright piercing through the canvas of darkness painted with the twinkling stars. Around midnight, they gathered their things and headed to their separate rooms. In the hallway, there were multiple rounds of hugs, kisses as well as an agreement that their next visit would have new sleeping arrangements along with new last names.

Jillian and Vernice were tucked in their beds and the lights were out. Vernice said, "Girl, would you have believed two years ago that you would be engaged to Byron and I would be dating Myron?"

"Never in my wildest dreams. God truly has a sense of humor," Jillian said.

"I still can't believe that you took me in that store today to try on rings. Are you kidding me?" Vernice asked.

"No, I am not kidding you because I was there," Jillian laughed, "Just enjoy it. Believe you me, you are going to have enough people mad because you are blessed."

"Exactly. Good night girl."

"Good night to you too."

Julia A. Royston

Vernice

Chapter 9

The next day was an early start with breakfast at 7:00 a.m. prior to the arrival of the staff from Indianapolis, Cincinnati and Dayton. Because of the holiday, everyone arrived on time so they could leave on time. Vernice and Jillian were proud and honored to be introduced to the team as consultants. Byron and Myron gave presentations on the vision for the future products and services. Each department head gave their presentation with needs assessments that matched Vernice and Jillian's expertise. By the end of the day, the team was convinced of the retention of Vernice and Jillian's services. Byron and Myron knew they had made the right decision in their personal as well as professional lives.

It was 4:00 p.m. and the team left. The four of them remained for one more night to unwind and enjoy the scenery. Myron and Vernice decided to take a walk through the woods.

"So I have to ask," Vernice said.

"Anything." Myron replied.

"Where do you see yourself in five years?" Vernice asked.

"In five years, I will be 45. I see the company continuing to grow. My role will be oversee research and development, but let my team do what they are qualified to do. Personally, I see myself married to you, loving you and helping you to grow into the business woman you want to be. I also want to be there to celebrate David's accomplishments in his life."

"Thank you. That makes me so happy. Yes, I'm going to cry," Vernice stopped on the trail and the tears flowed.

"It's okay to cry because I know that those are happy tears," Myron held her close and wiped her tears with his shirt. They swayed back and forth to the breeze through the trees and watched the sun going down.

"I've made your shirt a mess."

"That's no problem, water will dry. Tell me where you want to be in five years."

"First, being loved by you. Second, David, Jr. a college graduate and living his life. Third, I can't believe what I'm about to say, but own a thriving marketing and promotional firm 'Thompson Media Group.' Today, I enjoyed being a consultant. I am proud of my experience and what I know. I am learning a lot, but there is so much that I am qualified to bring to the table."

"I glad that you are finally accepting your new business course and you know I will help you. That's what love does and you know that I love you," She laughed which made Myron laugh as well.

"Yes, you do love me and I love you too," Vernice said.

"Now, I have another question for you, what about your mother? Do you think she would leave Chicago if you left?" Myron asked.

"My mother will probably never leave Chicago, but I'll ask her. You travel so much, where do you want to call home?" Vernice asked.

"My clothes are in Indianapolis. My heart is wherever you are so it doesn't matter. Byron is going to be in Cincinnati and Dayton so it doesn't matter where I live." Myron stated.

"Honestly, I don't have anything keeping me in Chicago. I can visit my mother anytime," Vernice said thoughtfully.

"Let's pray about it and see where that leads. Agreed?"

"I agree," Vernice said softly.

Vernice

Myron and Vernice sealed it with a kiss and continued to explore nature and discuss their life together.

The Retreat Center hosted a BBQ that night and once they were full, they sat around the fire watching the stars and listening to nature. Myron and Vernice had been dating only a short time, but in Myron's mind, it had been years in the making. He was not going to wait another second to make Vernice officially his.

Myron stood and knelt down in the front of the rocking chair where Vernice was sitting. Jillian saw him and tapped Byron's arm.

"Here he goes," whispered Jillian.

"Vernice, I love you," Myron said quietly.

"I love you too Myron," Vernice replied with water in her eyes.

"I want the world to know just how much I love you and want to spend the rest of my life with you. Will you marry me?" Myron asked.

Vernice began to cry and said, "Yes!" through her tears. Myron opened the blue box.

"It's the ring!" Vernice shouted as she looked up at Jillian who was wiping away her own tears comforted by Byron.

"No you didn't buy that ring!" Vernice yelled.

"Yes, I did buy that ring!" Myron exclaimed.

"You told him Jillian didn't you? Oh my goodness," Vernice was torn between excitement, frustration, embarrassment and pure joy. She knew how much the ring cost and she didn't think she deserved it.

"Yes I told him. Vernice you loved it so much and you deserve it." Jillian confessed.

"Yes, I did love it, but girl really?" Vernice said.

"Just say thank you Vernice," Jillian insisted.

Vernice

"Thank you Vernice," Vernice said while smiling through even more tears. They all laughed once again and all of the other guests nearby cheered for the newly engaged couple.

"Would you please give me your hand young lady?" Myron teased.

"Oh my goodness, Lord I can't take it." Vernice held out her hand and Myron slid the beautiful ring on her finger making it official. Myron stood, embraced and kissed her. Jillian and Byron were proud to witness the act of love. A group hug ensued. The ring glistened even in the twilight.

The next morning, the four headed to the 11:30 service of Jillian's church. Jillian and Vernice thought their hearts would burst from knowing that they would be sisters in law for life. The joy would be short lived as soon as they came into the front door of the church. Jillian was peeking through the sanctuary doors to see where they should sit when she was spotted by Sis. Wanda, the lead usher. Sis. Wanda had the unique ability to look forward, side to side and backward all at the same time.

"Sis. Jillian, you are late for church. Have you been out all night partying?" Sis. Wanda asked as she looked Jillian up, down and around again. Vernice was standing a few feet away waiting for Byron and Myron to come in from parking the car.

"I'm sorry but my mother is in the sanctuary already. It is great to see you too, Sis. Wanda," Jillian replied somewhat agitated.

Sis. Wanda turned her attention toward Vernice, "Good morning Sis. Vernice and welcome to New Life. What brings you to town?"

"Remember today is Jillian's bridal shower," Vernice replied.

Vernice

"Oh, that's right. So you came in town for your friend's shower. Bless the Lord, bless the Lord." Just then Myron and Byron came inside the door. Not realizing that Jillian and Vernice were with them, Sis. Wanda closed the door of the sanctuary and ran toward them, "Praise the Lord! It's both of the Randolph twins in the house today! Hallelujah! I realize that Bro. Byron is already taken by Sis. Jillian over there, but Bro. Myron is still available. I must alert the Sisters in Zion!"

"Good morning Sis. Wanda," the Randolph twins said matter-of-factly and in perfect unison as they had done all of their lives.

"I hate to diminish your excitement Sis. Wanda, but I am no longer available either. I just became engaged to Sis. Vernice on last evening." Myron said as he took Vernice's hand to show her the ring. Vernice stood there and smiled, no words were necessary.

Jillian came close and whispered, "Sis. Wanda, now run and tell that." Jillian took Byron's hand and the four laughed leaving Sis. Wanda standing in the lobby. They headed down the left aisle to a half empty pew in the nearly filled sanctuary. Jillian's two friends, Pamela and Linda, smiled and waved from the choir loft. Next was a song and the announcement about Jillian and Byron's wedding in July. The entire church applauded as Jillian and Byron stood. Next was "fellowship time," "pass the love" or as Byron called it, "get a little closer so I can be nosier" time.

The minister announced, "Now is one of my favorite times in the service, where we turn to our neighbor or reach across the aisle to say, God loves you and so do I."

"Here they come," Byron whispered in Jillian's ear which always made her laugh. Byron always managed to speak so close that he would blow air into her ear which always tickled.

Congratulations was extended by most who approached, but there were some long stares, inquisitive looks and interesting whispers. One of the senior members asked, "Vernice, you ain't dating the light skinned Randolph are you?"

"No ma'am I am not just dating Myron, we're engaged."

"Well, good Lord, I guess it's congratulations to you too. Well, two good church boys are taken off of the market by two great girls. God be praised."

"Thank you." Vernice replied with a smile.

Jillian had warned Vernice and she was ready for it.

Montgomery Inn was the dinner spot and also the site of the bridal shower. As they were riding to the restaurant, Vernice received a text from David, 'we're at the airport and I love you.'

Vernice called David right away. "David."

"Hey mom."

"You be good and have a great time."

"I will mom, love you."

"Love you always."

Myron put his hand through the opening between the seats and held Vernice's hand to reassure her that everything was going to be alright. Vernice caught a tear with her other hand.

At the restaurant, the ribs were delicious, the side dishes were divine and the company was even better. At exactly 3:00 p.m., the guys said 'goodbye and encouraged them both to have fun.' There were fifty women who began arriving at 3:30 p.m. for the bridal shower filled with presents, games, prizes and a huge cake.

The evening brought them all back to Byron's place to unload all of the beautiful presents Jillian received, change into comfortable clothes and lounge in the theatre room. Vernice and Myron realized that two people can fit nicely on one lounge chair.

After a nap, Myron turned on the TV to breaking news and a text on his phone that an American Airlines plane went down in the ocean right off the coast of the Bahamas. Myron turned to Vernice trying not to alarm her and asked, "Vernice, do you know what airline David was on to the Bahamas?"

"Yes, American Airlines, why?"

"What was his flight number?"

"Flight 567, why?"

"Text him."

"Myron you are scaring me. What's up?" Vernice's eyes got wide and filled with water.

"Vernice, baby, stay calm. I just got a text that there was trouble with an American Airlines flight."

Just then CNN broke through on the TV with a News Alert about a plane crash of American Airlines flight 567 and that all family members should contact a special number. Vernice called David's phone and it was going into answering. She tried texting, but he didn't answer. She called all of the Sanders' phone numbers that she knew, but there was no answer.

Vernice screamed, "No, not my baby! No, Jill no! Make the pain go away! I knew that my life was going too good. God no!! God no!! Myron help! Please baby help! Fix it!" Jillian held Vernice while she screamed and cried.

Myron and Byron hurried into a back bedroom to call the 800 number. Hearing Vernice's screams made Myron so nervous he couldn't dial the phone. He paced back and forth crying quietly while Byron dialed the number and waited for someone to answer, "Ma'am, calling about the

Vernice

flight 567 are there any survivors?" There was a short pause, "No, are you sure? Oh God no!" Myron screamed, "What Byron? No survivors! Jesus no! God please!"

The lady answering the phone was apologetic but asked for a cell phone to contact them. Byron remembered that Vernice had thrown her phone across the room when she could not reach her son. Thirty minutes later, Byron's phone buzzed in his hand. He didn't recognize the number, but he knew that he needed to answer it, "Hello, I have a family emergency so can you make it brief?"

"I'm sorry, but is Mr. Myron there?" a young voice said on the other line.

"Who is this?" Byron asked.

"David Washington, Vernice Washington's son," David, Jr. answered.

"Myron this is David on the phone!" Byron yelled.

"On the phone?" grabbing the phone from Byron, "David, where are you son?"

"We are still in Miami. We just got back into the airport from being on the runway for an hour. We can't go to Bahamas because of some crash and waiting on our luggage," David was touched that Mr. Myron called him son, but he would figure that out later.

"Hold on son," Myron ran down the hall yelling, "David's on the phone!"

"What!? David's on the phone?" Vernice grabbed the phone from Myron and he held on to her as she was yelling and crying, "David are you okay? David are you okay?"

"Mom, I am fine. We didn't go to the Bahamas. When I last texted you, Bishop Sanders forgot his wallet at the church. We didn't want to leave without him so we had to stay until the next flight. We changed our flight, but they won't let us go to

Vernice

Bahamas now because of the crash. The time share company got us a condo here in Miami."

"Oh baby, it is so great to hear your voice. I have been losing my mind thinking that you died in that plane crash."

"No, mom I'm fine. I guess you are right. God looks out for us."

"Yes, baby he does. I love you so much."

"I love you too mom. I'll send you pictures of the condo that we are staying in. Hey mom, Mr. Myron called me son twice."

"How do you feel about that?" Vernice asked looking at Myron quickly and smiling.

"It sounded so cool. I didn't want to embarrass him or myself over the phone, but I've got to talk to him when I get back home. Okay mom?" David, Jr. asked.

"That's fine with me. Anything you want David. Anything you want."

"By the way, mom, my phone was in airplane mode so I couldn't get your call if you tried to call me earlier. I've never been to Miami so... Myron stood close and watched Vernice as she listened to her son's every word. Vernice looked at Myron knowing that he had as much love and concern for her son as she did. Myron wiped his eyes just thinking about the possible loss of this great kid. Vernice cried even more looking at Myron. She finally said goodbye to David, Jr. and hugged Myron tight while kissing him frequently. She apologized for screaming and breaking her phone. She also thanked him for doing all he could and God for watching over her baby. Myron was thankful too. Byron and Jillian held each other tight and wiped away tears of joy knowing just how quick our loved ones can be taken away.

"Vernice you are fine. Scream and cry all you want. I'm just glad that he is alright. I'm still trying to figure out how he got Byron's phone number?" Myron asked.

Byron answered, "That wasn't my phone that was yours Myron. In all of the excitement, you handed me your phone. Right now it doesn't matter. David is safe, alive and we can move forward. Not to normal, but move forward."

"You got that right. Nothing will ever be the same after this. I got to get a new phone because I broke mine being mad. I don't think I've ever been that scared before," Vernice said.

Myron stayed with Vernice the rest of the night. She read the texts over and over that he sent her on Myron's phone right before they went to bed. She still woke several times with startling nightmares that David really was hurt. Myron reassured her over and over that David was safe and sound in Florida.

Monday morning it was the ladies' turn to spoil their men.

"I don't know much about cooking, but from the looks of this refrigerator there is nothing in here to cook," Jillian said.

"Girl, to the store we go," Vernice replied. Jillian's back seat was packed with groceries. The bacon, sausage, potatoes, eggs and toast was an alarm clock to the Randolph men. They took turns yelling how thankful they were for the breakfast. Byron was usually the clown, but this time it was Myron who sounded like a Baptist preacher on church anniversary raving about the good food.

Monday evening, Vernice said tearful goodbyes to Byron and Jillian. She knew that she would see them again at their wedding in six weeks, but she was still emotional from the weekend. Vernice almost missed her flight hugging, kissing and thanking Myron for everything. When she finally took her seat, she texted Myron and David, Jr. while looking at her ring.

The next day, Vernice's desk had two empty brown boxes on it and a note to report to Phillip Bennett's office. Vernice went to Phillip Bennett's office and he was seated at his desk and Janice was seated in an adjacent chair.

"Vernice you were warned about a personal relationship with a client and its apparent you ignored the warning. Here is a picture of you in the arms of Mr. Myron Randolph." Vernice looked at the picture and it was true. "You are being terminated from Wallace and Bennett immediately and please put whatever remaining personal items in those two boxes on your desk and you will be escorted out in 30 minutes."

"Goodbye." Vernice stood, turned on her heels and went back to her desk. There was nothing on her desk to take with her. All of her personal artifacts were safely in the third bedroom at her home. She got her purse and walked that long hallway to the front lobby with people watching from the doorways of their offices. She was normally a cry baby, but she was all cried out. She waited for the elevator, walked on and pushed the button for the first floor. The elevator was going down but her life was going up. She called her attorney on the way home on the bus. Once she got home, she called Myron.

"Hey baby."

"You okay? What's wrong?" Myron asked.

"They fired me."

"Today? What happened?"

"Someone took a picture of us a week ago and sent it to Phillip."

Vernice

"Okay, it happened somewhat like you thought. What's your next move?" Myron asked.

"I really want to get back on that plane and come back to you."

"Come on."

"Thanks so much. I'd love to, but I have to get my business straight here first. I am home and calm surprisingly, no screaming, no yelling, nothing just calm. Why I am so calm, I don't know?"

"I do because you saw it coming and even though you don't have a final plan, you have a plan. I would love to keep talking, but I have a meeting in an hour to get ready for. I love you and we will talk in about an hour."

"I love you too. Take your time because I am at home working." Vernice hung up the phone and called Charles Wallace.

Charles answered on the third ring, "Hello."

"Hello Charles, this is Vernice."

"Hello Vernice. Is this a new number? What's going on?"

"Well, yes, it is a new number and yes, they fired me today."

"On what grounds?"

"The same grounds that you warned me about over a month ago. Dating a client."

"First of all, Myron Randolph nor Randolph Technologies was under contract as a client of Wallace. We only made a presentation to him. Secondly, you may have a case against Wallace and Bennett. Third, I think I have a case against them too. Have you spoken with a lawyer?"

"I did before I left last week. I was told to keep my nose clean and wait until something else happened. That something has happened. I made an appointment for Thursday at 10."

"Well now you have to wait. In the meantime, get some research done. Work on your business plan and let me know what happens after you talk to your lawyer."

"Will do."

Vernice worked from home and the weeks following on Thompson Media Group. Vernice and Myron were in constant communication making their life plans. With tons of frequent flyer miles, Myron came to Chicago on Thursday to meet with her and her lawyer about the next steps. David, Jr. came home a week later to very tight hugs from his mother, Myron and his grandmother who returned from her trip as well. Vernice and Myron broke the news to David, Jr. and his grandmother about their engagement which made them all excited. David asked Myron one thing, "Can I call you dad and not Mr. Myron after you marry my mom?"

"You sure? You have a father and I don't want to take anything away from him."

"Mr. Myron, you know my dad is no good and I really liked it when you called me son on the phone twice last week."

"Well then, it is left up to your mother. What do you think Vernice?"

She burst into tears as normal saying, "I'm speechless. David is eighteen years old. If he wants to call you dad that is fine with me."

"Then it's settled. Dad it is." Myron and David did the manly hug and handshake. Vernice and her mother hugged and cried.

Vernice had so many decisions to make about her new business, old job, new marriage, her mother and son that it was scary, exciting and hectic all at the same time. Vernice knew that all aspects of her life would be changing, but the future was bright.

The week prior to the July 4th holiday, Vernice received a call from her lawyer, "Ms. Washington?"

Vernice

"Yes, hello Mr. Franklin. How are you?"

"I am fine. I have some good news and great news for you."

"What is that?"

"I received word back from Wallace and Bennett's lawyers that they have agreed to settle the wrongful termination case."

"Isn't that fast?"

"Yes, extremely fast. They have so many cases that they agreed to settle."

"That's good! What's the great news?"

"The great news is that they settled for $500,000 instead of the $100,000 we initially asked for."

Vernice nearly fainted. "I'm sorry Mr. Franklin I have to sit down. Did you say $500,000 or a half of a million dollars!?"

"Yes!"

"Hold on let me call my fiancé." Vernice dialed Myron's number and conferenced him in. "Myron?

Mr. Franklin? Great, you are both on the call.

"What's up baby?"

"Mr. Franklin tell my fiancé what you just told me."

Mr. Thomas Franklin relayed the message again and Myron was thrilled. Vernice said, "Now, I don't need to borrow money for my business. I have enough to start up, save and invest. Yes, Lord!"

"Minus my 30% of course," her attorney added.

"Well, of course, but I can do something with the balance."

"Yes, you can Ms. Washington. Have a great day Mr. Randolph."

"You too Mr. Franklin."

Chapter 10

Vernice's mom, Ms. Frances, David, Jr. and Vernice were on a plane to Cincinnati for Byron and Jillian's wedding. All of the bridal party was assembled in the church sanctuary for the wedding rehearsal along with Ms. Erma Jamison, the godmother to Vernice and Jillian from Houston, TX.

"Looks like you young girls have been busy falling in love, getting engaged and about to get married," Ms. Erma said.

"Yes, ma'am we are." Vernice showed Ms. Erma her ring and Sis. Erma compared it to Jillian's.

"Girl, them Randolph boys are something else. You should have warned me to get my sunglasses for the light from all of this bling, bling like the kids say," Ms. Erma said with a giggle.

"God has done some marvelous things in the short months since convention in March. Too many to name," Vernice said beaming.

"He will do it, if you let him. God is an awesome God," declared Ms. Erma. They all laughed and continued to enjoy each other's company. The coordinators of the wedding were clip board ready and completed the run through of the wedding program at least 3 times in one and a half hours in preparation for the next day. The Fellowship Hall of the church was the site for the rehearsal dinner. Ms. Ida Mae Washington walked in to the room and spotted someone very familiar. "Well, look who it is, Erma Jamison all the way from Houston." "You know I'm old and trying to go to heaven so stay far away from me Ida Mae Washington." Ms. Ida Mae leaned in close to Ms. Erma and said, "After all these years, you still going to hold that against me Erma?"

"You better believe I am. You had no right to ruin my life and chances at happiness years ago."

Vernice

"Are you kidding me? You never married anybody else after."

"You knew that was the love of my life after my husband died. Get away from me. If you won't leave me, I'm getting some fresh air."

Jillian and Vernice noticed the exchange and Vernice told Jillian that she would check on her. Vernice walked outside and found Ms. Erma sitting on the bench crying.

"You okay Ms. Erma?"

"I'm fine baby. I just wish she would just leave me alone. She has done enough to ruin my life."

"What did she do?"

"Nothing baby. I have held it in this long. I can hold it a bit longer. I don't want nothing to spoil Jillian's day. Go back in and I'll be there in a minute." Ms. Erma dried her eyes on her skirt as she had so long ago and said, "Lord help me get through these next few days, if only for my goddaughter's sake."

The rest of the night went without a hiccup. There was one big slumber party at Jillian's condo. It was five minutes to midnight and Byron called one more time to tell Jillian how much he loved her and couldn't wait to say 'I do' the next day. She said that she loved him back and they hung up the phone. Vernice, Ms. Erma, Ms. Frances and Jillian's mama, Ms. Doris were bound and determined that Byron could have no contact with Jillian until he saw her at the altar at 2:00 p.m. the next day.

The bridal party arrived at the church at 11:00 a.m. to dress and take pictures. The heavens opened up with a rain shower at noon and miraculously stopped at 1:30 p.m. Fortunately no one got wet except some early guests. The wedding started at exactly 2:00 p.m. The Maid of Honor was Vernice, Matron of Honor was Jillian's sister, Monica and

Vernice

the other bridesmaids were Pamela and Linda. Ms. Doris, Jillian's mother, sat on the front left pew alone. Mrs. Randolph sat on the right pew alone because Bishop Randolph was the officiant and Myron was the Best Man. The bridesmaids were dressed in long flowing yellow dresses and the groomsmen were exquisite in navy blue tuxedos. The bride and groom were styled in matching white dress and tuxedo. The vows were said, rings were exchanged, the last prayer was prayed and the couple kissed a kiss so long that it took Jillian's breath away.

Vernice looked at Myron, he gave her a huge wink and she mouthed, "I love you."

Myron mouthed back, "I love you more and you are next." Vernice wiped yet another tear with her custom made handkerchief.

The wedding party arrived to a private mansion overlooking the Ohio River with decorations that were breathtaking.

All was right with the world. Jillian Forrester was married to Byron Randolph. Vernice Washington was engaged and soon to be married to Myron Randolph. David Washington, Jr. would soon have a dad, not just a father. The Randolph Family was ecstatic.

At the reception, a very distinguished gentleman walked toward Ms. Erma Jamison, the godmother of Vernice and Jillian. He was a stately man with a beautiful black suit and red tie. He stood more than six feet tall with brown skin and light brown eyes.

He asked, "Erma is that you?"

Vernice

Erma turned toward the voice and said, "Yes, I'm sorry I don't know…." Ms. Erma stopped, blinked her eyes and thought, 'could it be?'

"Robert is that you?" Ms. Erma asked with a hoarse voice on the brink of tears.

Robert answered, "Yes it is."

About the Author

Julia Royston is an author, publisher, speaker, teacher and songwriter residing in Southern Indiana with her husband, Brian K. Royston. To her credit, Julia has written original music for 5 Music CDs, 2 DVDs, authored 20 Books, a contributing author in 3 books. Julia and her husband spend their spare time overseeing the operations of 3 companies and a non-profit organization. BK Royston Publishing, LLC and Royal Media Publishing to provide quality, informative, inspirational and entertaining materials in the global market place in all media formats. Julia Royston Enterprises is a writing and business consulting firm to assist aspiring authors and business owners get their message to the masses. For the Kingdom Ministries is a non-profit organization that is established to encourage, enlighten and empower people to live the abundant life and walk in purpose and destiny. By profession, Julia is a certified, technology teacher with the local public school system. For more information visit www.bkroystonpublishing.com, www.juliaroystonenterprises.com   or www.juliaroyston.net.

Vernice

Keep up with Julia on Social Media by following or liking her pages on Facebook, Twitter, LinkedIn, Instagram and Periscope.